Pictures
of
Sweden

Pictures of Sweden

Hans Christian Andersen

Author of:
"The Improvisatore," & c.

MANOR
Rockville, Maryland
2008

ISBN: 978-1-60450-179-7

Published by Arc Manor
P. O. Box 10339
Rockville, md 20849-0339
www.ArcManor.com

Printed in the United States of America/United Kingdom

Contents

Introduction

WE TRAVEL

༄

It is a delightful spring: the birds warble, but you do not understand their song? Well, hear it in a free translation.

"Get on my back," says the stork, our green island's sacred bird, "and I will carry thee over the Sound. Sweden also has fresh and fragrant beech woods, green meadows and corn-fields. In Scania, with the flowering apple-trees behind the peasant's house, you will think that you are still in Denmark."

"Fly with me," says the swallow; "I fly over Holland's mountain ridge, where the beech-trees cease to grow; I fly further towards the north than the stork. You shall see the vegetable mould pass over into rocky ground; see snug, neat towns, old churches and mansions, where all is good and comfortable, where the family stand in a circle around the table and say grace at meals, where the least of the children says a prayer, and, morning and evening, sings a psalm. I have heard it, I have seen it, when little, from my nest under the eaves."

"Come with me! come with me!" screams the restless sea-gull, and flies in an expecting circle. "Come with me to the Skjaer-gaards, where rocky isles by thousands, with fir and pine, lie like flower-beds along the coast; where the fishermen draw the well-filled nets!"

"Rest thee between our extended wings," sing the wild swans. "Let us bear thee up to the great lakes, the perpetually roaring elvs (rivers), that rush on with arrowy swiftness; where the oak forest has long ceased, and the birch-tree becomes stunted. Rest thee between our extended wings: we fly up to Sulitelma, the island's eye, as the mountain is called; we fly from the vernal green valley, up over the snow-drifts, to the mountain's top, whence thou canst see the North Sea, on yonder side of Norway.

"We fly to Jemteland, where the rocky mountains are high and blue; where the Foss roars and rushes; where the torches are lighted as *budstikke*[a] to announce that the ferryman is expected. Up to the deep, cold-running waters, where the midsummer sun does not set; where the rosy hue of eve is that of morn."

That is the birds' song. Shall we lay it to heart? Shall we accompany them?—at least a part of the way. We will not sit upon the stork's back, or between the swans' wings. We will go forward with steam, and with horses—yes, also on our own legs, and glance now and then from reality, over the fence into the region of thought, which is always our near neighbour-land; pluck a flower or a leaf, to be placed in the note-book—for it sprung out during our journey's flight: we fly and we sing. Sweden, thou glorious land! Sweden, where, in ancient times, the sacred gods came from Asia's mountains! land that still retains rays of their lustre, which streams from the flowers in the name of "Linnaeus;" which beams for thy chivalrous men from Charles the Twelfth's banner; which sounds from the obelisk on the field of Lutzen! Sweden, thou land of deep feeling, of heart-felt songs! home of the limpid elvs, where the wild swans sing in the gleam of the Northern Lights! Thou land, on whose deep, still lakes Scandinavia's fairy builds her colonnades, and leads her battling, shadowy host over the icy mirror! Glorious Sweden! with thy fragrant Linnaeus, with Jenny's soul-enlivening songs! To thee will we fly with the stork and the swallow, with the restless sea-gull and the wild swans. Thy birch-woods exhale refreshing fragrance under their sober, bending branches; on the tree's white stem the harp shall hang: the North's summer wind shall whistle therein!

---

a A chip of wood in the form of a halberd, circulated for the purpose of convening the inhabitants of a district in Sweden and Norway.

Trollhaetta

⁂

Who did we meet at Trollhaetta? It is a strange story, and we will relate it.

We landed at the first sluice, and stood as it were in a garden laid out in the English style. The broad walks are covered with gravel, and rise in short terraces between the sunlit greensward: it is charming, delightful here, but by no means imposing. If one desires to be excited in this manner, one must go a little higher up to the older sluices, which deep and narrow have burst through the hard rock. It looks magnificent, and the water in its dark bed far below is lashed into foam. Up here one overlooks both elv and valley; the bank of the river on the other side, rises in green undulating hills, grouped with leafy trees and red-painted wooden houses, which are bounded by rocks and pine forests. Steam-boats and sailing vessels ascend through the sluices; the water itself is the attendant spirit that must bear them up above the rock, and from the forest itself it buzzes, roars and rattles. The din of Trollhaetta Falls mingles with the noise from the saw-mills and smithies.

"In three hours we shall be through the sluices," said the Captain: "in that time you will see the Falls. We shall meet again at the inn up here."

We went from the path through the forest: a whole flock of bare-headed boys surrounded us. They would all be our guides; the one screamed longer than the other, and every one gave his contradictory explanation, how high the water stood, and how high it did not stand, or could stand. There was also a great difference of opinion amongst the learned.

We soon stopped on a ling-covered rock, a dizzying terrace. Before us, but far below, was the roaring water, the Hell Fall, and over this again, fall after fall, the rich, rapid, rushing elv—the outlet of the largest lake in Sweden. What a sight! what a foaming and roaring, above—below! It is like the waves of the sea, but of effervescing champagne—of boiling milk. The water rushes round two rocky islands at the top so that the spray rises like meadow dew. Below, the water is more compressed, then hurries down again, shoots forward and returns in circles like smooth water, and then rolls darting its long sea-like fall into the Hell Fall. What a tempest rages in the deep—what a sight! Words cannot express it!

Nor could our screaming little guides. They stood mute; and when they again began with their explanations and stories, they did not come far, for an old gentleman whom none of us had noticed (but he was now amongst us), made himself heard above the noise, with his singularly sounding voice. He knew all the particulars about the place, and about former days, as if they had been of yesterday.

"Here, on the rocky holms," said he, "it was that the warriors in the heathen times, as they are called, decided their disputes. The warrior Staerkodder dwelt in this district, and liked the pretty girl Ogn right well; but she was fonder of Hergrimmer, and therefore he was challenged by Staerkodder to combat here by the falls, and met his death; but Ogn sprung towards them, took her bridegroom's bloody sword, and thrust it into her own heart. Thus Staerkodder did not gain her. Then there passed a hundred years, and again a hundred years: the forests were then thick and closely grown; wolves and bears prowled here summer and winter; the place was infested with malignant robbers, whose hiding-place no one could find. It was yonder, by the fall before Top Island, on the Norwegian side—there was their cave: now it has fallen in! The cliff there overhangs it!"

"Yes, the Tailor's Cliff!" shouted all the boys. "It fell in the year 1755!"

"Fell!" said the old man, as if in astonishment that any one but himself could know it. "Everything will fall once, and the tailor directly." The robbers had placed him upon the cliff and demanded that if he would be liberated from them, his ransom should be that he should sew a suit of clothes up there; and he tried it; but at the first stitch, as he drew the thread out, he became giddy and fell down into the gushing water, and thus the rock got the name of 'The Tailor's Cliff.' One day the robbers caught a young girl, and she betrayed them, for she kindled a fire in the cavern. The smoke was seen, the caverns discovered, and the robbers imprisoned and executed. That outside there is called 'The Thieves' Fall,' and down there under the water is another cave, the elv rushes in there and returns boiling; one can see it well up here, one hears it too, but it can be heard better under the bergman's loft.

And we went on and on, along the Fall, towards Top Island, continuously on smooth paths covered with saw-dust, to Polham's Sluice. A cleft had been made in the rock for the first intended sluice-work, which was not finished, but whereby art has created the most imposing of all Trollhaetta's Falls; the hurrying water falling here perpendicularly into the black deep. The side of the rock is here placed in connection with Top Island by means of a light iron bridge, which appears as if thrown over the abyss. We venture on to the rocking bridge over the streaming, whirling water, and then stand on the little cliff island, between firs and pines, that shoot forth from the crevices. Before us darts a sea of waves, which are broken by the rebound against the stone block where we stand, bathing us with the fine spray. The torrent flows on each side, as if shot out from a gigantic cannon, fall after fall: we look out over them all, and are filled with the harmonic sound, which since time began, has ever been the same.

"No one can ever get to the island there," said one of our party, pointing to the large island above the topmost fall.

"I however know one!" said the old man, and nodded with a peculiar smile.

"Yes, my grandfather could!" said one of the boys, "scarcely any one besides has crossed during a hundred years. The cross that is set up over there was placed there by my grandfather. It had been a severe winter, the whole of Lake Venern was frozen; the ice dammed up the outlet, and for many hours there was a dry bottom. Grandfather has told about it: he went over with two others, placed the cross up, and returned. But then there was such a thundering and cracking noise, just as if it were cannons. The ice broke up and the elv came over the fields and forest. It is true, every word I say!"

One of the travellers cited Tegner:

> *"Vildt Goeta stortade fran Fjallen,*
> *Hemsk Trollet fran sat Toppfall roet!*
> *Men Snillet kom och spraengt stod Hallen,*
> *Med Skeppen i sitt skoet!"*

"Poor mountain sprite," he continued, "thy power and glory recede! Man flies over thee—thou mayst go and learn of him."

The garrulous old man made a grimace, and muttered something to himself—but we were just by the bridge before the inn. The steam-boat glided through the opened way, every one hastened to get on board, and it directly shot away above the Fall, just as if no Fall existed.

"And that can be done!" said the old man. He knew nothing at all about steam-boats, had never before that day seen such a thing, and accordingly he was sometimes up and sometimes down, and stood by the machinery and stared at the whole construction, as if he were counting all the pins and screws. The course of the canal appeared to him to be something quite new; the plan of it and the guide-books were quite foreign objects to him: he turned them and turned them—for read I do not think he could. But he knew all the particulars about the country—that is to say, from olden times.

I heard that he did not sleep at all the whole night. He studied the passage of the steam-boat; and when we in the morning ascended the sluice terraces from Lake Venern, higher and higher from lake to lake, away over the high-plain—higher, continually higher—he was in such activity that it appeared as if it could not be greater—and then we reached Motala.

The Swedish author Tjoerneroes relates of himself, that when a child he once asked what it was that ticked in the clock, and they answered him that it was one named *"Bloodless."* What brought the child's pulse to beat with feverish throbs and the hair on his head to rise, also exercised its power in Motala, over the old man from Trollhaetta.

We now went through the great manufactory in Motala. What ticks in the clock, beats here with strong strokes of the hammer. It is *Bloodless*, who drank life from human thought and thereby got limbs of metals, stone and wood; it is *Bloodless*, who by human thought gained strength, which man himself does not physically possess.

Bloodless reigns in Motala, and through the large foundries and factories he extends his hard limbs, whose joints and parts consist of wheel within wheel, chains, bars, and thick iron wires. Enter, and see how the glowing iron masses are formed into long bars. *Bloodless* spins the glowing bar! see how the shears cut into the heavy metal plates; they cut as quietly and as softly as if the plates were paper. Here where he hammers, the sparks fly from the anvil. See how he breaks the thick iron bars; he breaks them into lengths; it is as if it were a stick of sealing-wax that is broken. The long iron bars rattle before your feet; iron plates are planed into shavings; before you rolls the large wheel, and above your head runs living wire—long heavy wire! There is a hammering and buzzing, and if you look around in the large open yard, amongst great up-turned copper boilers, for steam-boats and locomotives, *Bloodless* also here stretches out one of his fathom-long fingers, and hauls away. Everything is living; man alone stands and is silenced by—*stop!*

The perspiration oozes out of one's fingers'-ends: one turns and turns, bows, and knows not one's self, from pure respect for the human thought which here has iron limbs. And yet the large iron hammer goes on continually with its heavy strokes: it is as if it said: "Banco, Banco! many thousand dollars; Banco, pure gain! Banco! Banco!"—Hear it, as I heard it; see, as I saw!

The old gentleman from Trollhaetta walked up and down in full contemplation; bent and swung himself about; crept on his knees, and stuck his head into corners and between the machines, for he would know everything so exactly; he would see the screw in the propelling vessels, understand their mechanism and effect under water—and the water itself poured like hail-drops down his forehead. He fell unconscious, backwards into my arms, or else he would have been drawn into the machinery, and been crushed: he looked at me, and pressed my hand.

"And all this goes on naturally," said he; "simply and comprehensibly. Ships go against the wind, and against the stream, sail higher than forests and mountains. The water must raise, steam must drive them!"

"Yes," said I.

"Yes," said he, and again *yes*, with a sigh which I did not then understand; but, months after, I understood it, and I will at once make a spring to that time, and we are again at Trollhaetta.

I came here in the autumn, on my return home; stayed some days in this mighty piece of nature, where busy human life forces its way more and more in, and, by degrees, transforms the picturesque to the useful manufactory. Trollhaetta must do her work; saw beams, drive mills, hammer and break to pieces: one building grows up by the side of the other, and in half a century hence here will be a city. But that was not the story.

I came, as I have said, here again in the autumn. I found the same rushing and roaring, the same din, the same rising and sinking in the sluices, the same chattering boys who conducted fresh travellers to the Hell Fall, to the iron-bridge island, and to the inn. I sat here, and turned over the leaves of books, collected here through a series of years, in which travellers have inscribed their names, feelings and thoughts at Trollhaetta—almost always the same astonishment, expressed in different languages, though generally in Latin: *veni, vidi, obstupui.*

One has written: "I have seen nature's master-piece pervade that of art;" another cannot say what he saw, and what he saw he cannot say. A mine owner and manufacturer, full of the doctrine of utility, has written: "Seen with the greatest pleasure this useful work for us in Vaermeland, Trollhaetta." The wife of a dean from Scania expresses herself thus. She has kept to the family, and only signed in the remembrance book, as to the effect of her feelings at Trollhaetta. "God grant my brother-in-law fortune, for he has understanding!" Some few have added witticisms to the others' feelings; yet as a pearl on this heap of writing shines Tegner's poem, written by himself in the book on the 28th of June, 1804:

"Gotha kom i dans fran Seves fjallar, &c."

I looked up from the book and who should stand before me, just about to depart again, but the old man from Trollhaetta! Whilst I had wandered about, right up to the shores of Siljan, he had continually made voyages on the canal; seen the sluices and manufactories, studied steam in all its possible powers of service, and spoke about a projected railway in Sweden, between the Hjalmar and Venern. He had, however, never yet seen a railway, and I described to him these extended roads, which sometimes rise like ramparts, sometimes like towering bridges, and at times like halls of miles in length, cut through rocks. I also spoke of America and England.

"One takes breakfast in London, and the same day one drinks tea in Edinburgh."

"That I can do!" said the man, and in as cool a tone as if no one but himself could do it, "I can also," said I; "and I have done it."

"And who are you, then?" he asked.

"A common traveller," I replied; "a traveller who pays for his conveyance. And who are you?"

The man sighed.

"You do not know me: my time is past; my power is nothing! *Bloodless* is stronger than I!" and he was gone.

I then understood who he was. Well, in what humour must a poor mountain sprite be, who only comes up every hundred years to see how things go forward here on the earth!

It was the mountain sprite and no other, for in our time every intelligent person is considerably wiser; and I looked with a sort of proud feeling on the present generation, on the gushing, rushing, whirling wheel, the heavy blows of the hammer, the shears that cut so softly through the metal plates, the thick iron bars that were broken like sticks of sealing-wax, and the music to which the heart's pulsations vibrate: "Banco, Banco, a hundred thousand Banco!" and all by steam—by mind and spirit.

It was evening. I stood on the heights of Trollhaetta's old sluices, and saw the ships with outspread sails glide away through the meadows like spectres, large and white. The sluice gates were opened with a ponderous and crashing sound, like that related of the copper gates of the secret council in Germany. The evening was so still that Trollhaetta's Fall was as audible in the deep stillness, as if it were a chorus from a hundred water-mills—ever one and the same tone. In one, however, there sounded a mightier crash that seemed to pass sheer through the earth; and yet with all this the endless silence of nature was felt. Suddenly a large bird flew out from the trees, far in the forest, down towards the Falls. Was it the mountain sprite?—We will imagine so, for it is the most interesting fancy.

THE BIRD PHOENIX

In the garden of Paradise, under the tree of knowledge, stood a hedge of roses. In the first rose a bird was hatched; its flight was like that of light, its colours beautiful, its song magnificent.

But when Eve plucked the fruit of knowledge, when she and Adam were driven from the garden of Paradise, a spark from the avenging angel's flaming sword fell into the bird's nest and kindled it. The bird died in the flames, but from the red egg there flew a new one—the only one—the ever only bird Phoenix. The legend states that it takes up its abode in Arabia; that every hundred years it burns itself up in its nest, and that a new Phoenix, the only one in the world, flies out from the red egg.

The bird hovers around us, rapid as the light, beautiful in colour, glorious in song. When the mother sits by the child's cradle, it is by the pillow, and with its wings flutters a glory around the child's head. It flies through the chamber of contentment, and there is the sun's radiance within:—the poor chest of drawers is odoriferous with violets.

But the bird Phoenix is not alone Arabia's bird: it flutters in the rays of the Northern Lights on Lapland's icy plains; it hops amongst the yellow flowers in Greenland's short summer. Under Fahlun's copper rocks, in England's coal mines, it flies like a powdered moth over the hymn-book in the pious workman's hands. It sails on the lotus-leaf down the sacred waters of the Ganges, and the eyes of the Hindoo girl glisten on seeing it.

The bird Phoenix! Dost thou not know it? The bird of Paradise, song's sacred swan! It sat on the car of Thespis, like a croaking raven, and flapped its black, dregs-besmeared wings; over Iceland's minstrel-harp glided the swan's red, sounding bill. It sat on Shakspeare's shoulder like Odin's raven, and whispered in his ear: "Immortality!" It flew at the minstrel competition, through Wartzburg's knightly halls.

The bird Phoenix! Dost thou not know it? It sang the Marseillaise for thee, and thou didst kiss the plume that fell from its wing: it came in the lustre of Paradise, and thou perhaps didst turn thyself away to some poor sparrow that sat with merest tinsel on its wings.

The bird of Paradise! regenerated every century, bred in flames, dead in flames; thy image set in gold hangs in the saloons of the rich, even though thou fliest often astray and alone. "The bird Phoenix in Arabia"—is but a legend.

In the garden of Paradise, when thou wast bred under the tree of knowledge, in the first rose, our Lord kissed thee and gave thee thy proper name—Poetry.

KINNAKULLA

Kinnakulla, Sweden's hanging gardens! Thee will we visit. We stand by the lowest terrace in a plenitude of flowers and verdure; the ancient village church leans its grey pointed wooden tower, as if it would fall; it produces an effect in the landscape: we would not even be without that large flock of birds, which just now chance to fly away over the mountain forest.

The high road leads up the mountain with short palings on either side, between which we see extensive plains with hops, wild roses, corn-fields, and delightful beech woods, such as are not to be found in any other place in Sweden. The ivy winds itself around old trees and stones—even to the withered trunk green leaves are lent. We look out over the flat, extended woody plain, to the sunlit church-tower of Maristad, which shines like a white sail on the dark green sea: we look out over the Venern Lake, but cannot see its further shore. Skjaergaardens' wood-crowned rocks lie like a wreath down in the lake; the steam-boat comes—see! down by the cliff under the red-roofed mansions, where the beech and walnut trees grow in the garden.

The travellers land; they wander under shady trees away over that pretty light green meadow, which is enwreathed by gardens and woods: no English park has a finer verdure than the meadows near Hellekis. They go up to "the grottos," as they call the projecting masses of red stone higher up, which, being thoroughly kneaded with petrifactions, project from the declivity of the earth, and remind one of the mouldering colossal tombs in the Campagna of Rome. Some are smooth and rounded off by the streaming of the water, others bear the moss of ages, grass and flowers, nay, even tall trees.

The travellers go from the forest road up to the top of Kinnakulla, where a stone is raised as the goal of their wanderings. The traveller reads in his guide-book about the rocky strata of Kinnakulla: "At the bottom is found sandstone, then alum-stone, then limestone, and above this red-stone, higher still slate, and lastly, trap." And, now that he has seen this, he descends again, and goes on board. He has seen Kinnakulla:—yes, the stony rock here, amidst the swelling verdure, showed him one heavy, thick stone finger, and most of the travellers think that they are like the devil, if they lay hold upon one finger, they have the body—but it is not always so. The least visited side of Kinnakulla is just the most characteristic, and thither will we go.

The road still leads us a long way on this side of the mountain, step by step downwards, in long terraces of rich fields: further down, the slate-stone peers forth in flat layers, a green moss upon it, and it looks like threadbare patches in the green velvet carpet. The high road leads over an extent of ground where the slate-stone lies like a firm floor. In the Campagna of Rome, one would say it is a piece of *via appia*, or antique road; but it is Kinnakulla's naked skin and bones that we pass over. The peasant's house is composed of large slate-stones, and the roof is covered with them; one sees nothing of wood except that of the door, and above it, of the large painted shield, which states to what regiment the soldier belongs who got this house and plot of ground in lieu of pay.

We cast another glance over Venern, to Lockoe's old palace, to the town of Lendkjobing, and are again near verdant fields and noble trees, that cast their shadows over Blomberg, where, in the garden, the poet Geier's spirit seeks the flower of Kinnakulla in his grand-daughter, little Anna.

The plain expands here behind Kinnakulla; it extends for miles around, towards the horizon. A shower stands in the heavens; the wind has increased: see how the rain falls to the ground like a darkening veil. The branches of the trees lash one another like penitential dryades. Old Husaby church lies near us, yonder; though the shower lashes the high walls, which alone stand, of the old Catholic Bishop's palace. Crows and ravens fly through the long glass-less windows, which time has made larger; the rain pours down the crevices in the old grey walls, as if they were now to be loosened stone from stone: but the church stands—old Husaby church—so grey and venerable, with its thick walls, its small windows, and its three spires stuck against each other, and standing, like nuts, in a cluster.

The old trees in the churchyard cast their shade over ancient graves. Where is the district's "Old Mortality," who weeds the grass, and explains the ancient memorials? Large granite stones are laid here in the form of coffins, ornamented with rude carvings from the times of Catholicism. The old church-door creaks in the hinges. We stand within its walls, where the vaulted roof was filled for centuries with the fragrance of incense, with monks, and with the song of the choristers. Now it is still and mute here: the old men in their monastic dresses have passed into their graves; the blooming boys that swung the censer are in their graves; the congregation—many generations—all in their graves; but the church still stands the same. The moth-eaten, dusty cowls, and the bishops' mantle, from the days of the cloister, hang in the old oak presses; and old manuscripts, half eaten up by the rats, lie strewed about on the shelves in the sacristy.

In the left aisle of the church there still stands, and has stood time out of mind, a carved image of wood, painted in various colours which are still strong: it is the Virgin Mary with the child Jesus. Fresh flower wreaths are hung around hers and the child's head; fragrant garlands are twined around the pedestal, as festive as on Madonna's birthday feast in the times of Popery. The young folks who have been confirmed, have this day, on receiving the sacrament for the first time, ornamented this old image—nay, even set the priest's name in flowers upon the altar; and he has, to our astonishment, let it remain there.

The image of Madonna seems to have become young by the fresh wreaths: the fragrant flowers here have a power like that of poetry—they bring back the days of past centuries to our own times. It is as if the extinguished glory around the head shone again; the flowers exhale perfume: it is as if incense again streamed through the aisles of the church—it shines around the altar as if the consecrated tapers were lighted—it is a sunbeam through the window.

The sky without has become clear: we drive again in under Cleven, the barren side of Kinnakulla: it is a rocky wall, different from almost all the others. The red stone blocks lie, strata on strata, forming fortifications with embrasures, projecting wings and round towers; but shaken, split and fallen in ruins—it is an architectural fantastic freak of nature. A brook falls gushing down from one of the highest points of the Cleven, and drives a little mill. It looks like a plaything which the mountain sprite had placed there and forgotten.

Large masses of fallen stone blocks lie dispersed round about; nature has spread them in the forms of carved cornices. The most significant way of describing Kinnakulla's rocky wall is to call it the ruins of a mile-long Hindostanee temple: these rocks might be easily transformed by the hammer into sacred places like the Ghaut mountains at Ellara. If a Brahmin were to come to Kinnakulla's rocky wall, he would recognise the temple of Cailasa, and find in the clefts and crevices whole representations from Ramagena and Mahabharata. If one should then speak to him in a sort of gibberish—no matter what, only that, by the help of Brockhaus's "Conversation-Lexicon" one might mingle therein the names of some of the Indian spectacles:—Sakantala, Vikramerivati, Uttaram Ramatscheritram, &c.—the Brahmin would be completely mystified, and write in his note-book: "Kinnakulla is the remains of a temple, like those we have in Ellara; and the inhabitants themselves know the most considerable works in our oldest Sanscrit literature, and speak in an extremely spiritual manner about them." But no Brahmin comes to the high rocky walls—not to speak of the company from the steam-boat, who are already far over the lake Venern. They have seen wood-crowned Kinnakulla, Sweden's hanging gardens—and we also have now seen them.

GRANDMOTHER

Grandmother is so old, she has so many wrinkles, and her hair is quite white; but her eyes! they shine like two stars, nay, they are much finer—they are so mild, so blissful to look into. And then she knows the most amusing stories, and she has a gown with large, large flowers on it, and it is of such thick silk that it actually rustles. Grandmother knows so much, for she has lived long before father and mother—that is quite sure.

Grandmother has a psalm-book with thick silver clasps, and in that book she often reads. In the middle of it lies a rose, which is quite flat and dry; but it is not so pretty as the roses she has in the glass, yet she smiles the kindliest to it, nay, even tears come into her eyes!

Why does Grandmother look thus on the withered flower in the old book? Do you know why?

Every time that Grandmother's tears fall on the withered flower the colours become fresher; the rose then swells and the whole room is filled with fragrance; the walls sink as if they were but mists; and round about, it is the green, the delightful grove, where the sun shines between the leaves. And Grandmother—yes, she is quite young; she is a beautiful girl, with yellow hair, with round red cheeks, pretty and charming—no rose is fresher. Yet the eyes, the mild, blissful eyes,—yes, they are still Grandmother's! By her side sits a man, young and strong: he presents the rose to her and she smiles. Yet grandmother does not smile so,—yes; the smile comes,—he is gone.—Many thoughts and many forms go past! That handsome man is gone; the rose lies in the psalm-book, and grandmother,—yes, she again sits like an old woman, and looks on the withered rose that lies in the book.

Now grandmother is dead!

She sat in the arm-chair, and told a long, long, sweet story. "And now it is ended!" said she, "and I am quite tired: let me now sleep a little!" And so she laid her head back to rest. She drew her breath, she slept, but it became more and more still; and her face was so full of peace and happiness—it was as if the sun's rays passed over it. She smiled, and then they said that she was dead.

She was laid in the black coffin; she lay swathed in the white linen: she was so pretty, and yet the eyes were closed—but all the wrinkles were gone. She lay with a smile around her mouth: her hair was so silvery white, so venerable, one was not at all afraid to look on the dead, for it was the sweet, benign grandmother. And the psalm-book was laid in the coffin under her head (she herself had requested it), and the rose lay in the old book—and then they buried grandmother.

On the grave, close under the church-wall, they planted a rose-tree, and it became full of roses, and the nightingale sang over it, and the organ in the church played the finest psalms that were in the book under the dead one's head. And the moon shone straight down on the grave—but the dead was not there: every child could go quietly in the night-time and pluck a rose there by the church-yard-wall. The dead know more than all we living know—the dead know the awe we should feel at something so strange as their coming to us. The dead are better than us all, and therefore they do not come.

There is earth over the coffin, there is earth within it; the psalm-book with its leaves is dust the rose with all its recollections has gone to dust. But above it bloom new roses, above is sings the nightingale, and the organ plays:—we think of the old grandmother with the mild, eternally young eyes. Eyes can never die! Ours shall once again see her young, and beautiful, as when she for the first time kissed the fresh red rose which is now dust in the grave.

The Prison-Cells

By separation from other men, by solitary confinement, in continual silence, the criminal is to be punished and amended; therefore were prison-cells contrived. In Sweden there were several, and new ones have been built. I visited one for the first time in Mariestad. This building lies close outside the town, by a running water, and in a beautiful landscape. It resembles a large white-washed summer residence, window above window.

But we soon discover that the stillness of the grave rests over it. It is as if no one dwelt here, or like a deserted mansion in the time of the plague. The gates in the walls are locked: one of them is opened for us: the gaoler stands with his bunch of keys: the yard is empty, but clean—even the grass weeded away between the stone paving. We enter the waiting-room, where the prisoner is received: we are shown the bathing-room, into which he is first led. We now ascend a flight of stairs, and are in a large hall, extending the whole length and breadth of the building. Galleries run along the floors, and between these the priest has his pulpit, where he preaches on Sundays to an invisible congregation. All the doors facing the gallery are half opened: the prisoners hear the priest, but cannot see him, nor he them. The whole is a well-built machine—a nightmare for the spirit. In the door of every cell there is fixed a glass, about the size of the eye: a slide covers it, and the gaoler can, unobserved by the prisoner, see everything he does; but he must come gently, noiselessly, for the prisoner's ear is wonderfully quickened by solitude. I turned the slide quite softly, and looked into the closed space, when the prisoner's eye immediately met mine. It is airy, clean, and light within the cell, but the window is placed so high that it is impossible to look out of it. A high stool, made fast to a sort of table, and a hammock, which can be hung upon hooks under the ceiling, and covered with a quilt, compose the whole furniture.

Several cells were opened for us. In one of these was a young, and extremely pretty girl. She had lain down in her hammock, but sprang out directly the door was opened, and her first employment was to lift her hammock down, and roll it together. On the little table stood a pitcher with water, and by it lay the remains of some oatmeal cakes, besides the Bible and some psalms.

In the cell close by sat a child's murderess. I saw her only through the little glass in the door. She had had heard our footsteps; heard us speak; but she sat still, squeezed up into the corner by the door, as if she would hide herself as much as possible: her back was bent, her head almost on a level with her lap, and her hands folded over it. They said this unfortunate creature was very young. Two brothers sat here in two different cells: they were punished for horse stealing; the one was still quite a boy.

In one cell was a poor servant girl. They said: "She has no place of resort, and without a situation, and therefore she is placed here." I thought I had not heard rightly, and repeated my question, "why she was here," but got the same answer. Still I would rather believe that I had misunderstood what was said—it would otherwise be abominable.

Outside, in the free sunshine, it is the busy day; in here it is always midnight's stillness. The spider that weaves its web down the wall, the swallow which perhaps flies a single time close under the panes there high up in the wall—even the stranger's footstep in the gallery, as he passes the cell-doors, is an event in that mute, solitary life, where the prisoners' thoughts are wrapped up in themselves. One must read of the martyr-filled prisons of the Inquisition, of the crowds chained together in the Bagnes, of the hot, lead chambers of Venice, and the black, wet gulf of the wells—be thoroughly shaken by these pictures of misery, that we may with a quieter pulsation of the heart wander through the gallery of the prison-cells. Here is light, here is air;—here it is more humane. Where the sunbeam shines mildly in on the prisoner, there also will the radiance of God shine into the heart.

Beggar-Boys

※※※

The painter Callot—who does not know the name, at least from Hoffmann's "in Callot's manner?"—has given a few excellent pictures of Italian beggars. One of these is a fellow, on whom the one rag lashes the other: he carries his huge bundle and a large flag with the inscription, "Capitano de Baroni." One does not think that there can in reality be found such a wandering rag-shop, and we confess that in Italy itself we have not seen any such; for the beggar-boy there, whose whole clothing often consists only of a waistcoat, has in it not sufficient costume for such rags.

But we see it in the North. By the canal road between the Venern and Vigen, on the bare, dry rocky plain there stood, like beauty's thistles in that poor landscape, a couple of beggar-boys, so ragged, so tattered, so picturesquely dirty, that we thought we had Callot's originals before us, or that it was an arrangement of some industrious parents, who would awaken the traveller's attention and benevolence. Nature does not form such things: there was something so bold in the hanging on of the rags, that each boy instantly became a Capitano de Baroni.

The younger of the two had something round him that had certainly once been the jacket of a very corpulent man, for it reached almost to the boy's ancles; the whole hung fast by a piece of the sleeve and a single brace, made from the seam of what was now the rest of the lining. It was very difficult to see the transition from jacket to trowsers, the rags glided so into one another. The whole clothing was arranged so as to give him an air-bath: there were draught holes on all sides and ends; a yellow linen clout fastened to the nethermost regions seemed as if it were to signify a shirt. A very large straw hat, that had certainly been driven over several times, was stuck sideways on his head, and allowed the boy's wiry, flaxen hair to grow freely through the opening where the crown should have been: the naked brown shoulder and upper part of the arm, which was just as brown, were the prettiest of the whole.

The other boy had only a pair of trowsers on. They were also ragged, but the rags were bound fast into the pockets with packthread; one string round the ancles, one under the knee, and another round about the waist. He, however, kept together what he had, and that is always respectable.

"Be off!" shouted the Captain, from the vessel; and the boy with the tied-up rags turned round, and we—yes, we saw nothing but packthread, in bows, genteel bows. The front part of the boy only was covered: he had only the foreparts of trowsers—the rest was packthread, the bare, naked packthread.

VADSTENE

❧

In Sweden, it is not only in the country, but even in several of the
provincial towns, that one sees whole houses of grass turf or with
roofs of grass turf; and some are so low that one might easily spring
up to the roof, and sit on the fresh greensward. In the early spring,
whilst the fields are still covered with snow, but which is melted on
the roof, the latter affords the first announcement of spring, with the
young sprouting grass where the sparrow twitters: "Spring comes!"

Between Motala and Vadstene, close by the high road, stands a
grass-turf house—one of the most picturesque. It has but one window, broader than it is high, and a wild rose branch forms the cur-
tain outside.

We see it in the spring. The roof is so delightfully fresh with
grass, it has quite the tint of velvet; and close to it is the chimney,
nay, even a cherry-tree grows out of its side, now full of flowers:
the wind shakes the leaves down on a little lamb that is tethered
to the chimney. It is the only lamb of the family. The old dame
who lives here, lifts it up to its place herself in the morning and
lifts it down again in the evening, to give it a place in the room.
The roof can just bear the little lamb, but not more—this is an experience and a certainty. Last autumn—and at that time the grass
turf roofs are covered with flowers, mostly blue and yellow, the
Swedish colours—there grew here a flower of a rare kind. It shone
in the eyes of the old Professor, who on his botanical tour came
past here. The Professor was quickly up on the roof, and just as
quick was one of his booted legs through it, and so was the other

leg, and then half of the Professor himself—that part where the head does not sit; and as the house had no ceiling, his legs hovered right over the old dame's head, and that in very close contact. But now the roof is again whole; the fresh grass grows where learning sank; the little lamb bleats up there, and the old dame stands beneath, in the low doorway, with folded hands, with a smile on her mouth, rich in remembrances, legends and songs, rich in her only lamb on which the cherry-tree strews its flower-blossoms in the warm spring sun.

As a background to this picture lies the Vettern—the bottomless lake as the commonalty believe—with its transparent water, its sea-like waves, and in calm, with "Hegring," or fata morgana on its steel-like surface. We see Vadstene palace and town, "the city of the dead," as a Swedish author has called it—Sweden's Herculaneum, reminiscence's city. The grass-turf house must be our box, whence we see the rich mementos pass before us—memorials from the chronicle of saints, the chronicle of kings and the love songs that still live with the old dame, who stands in her low house there, where the lamb crops the grass on the roof. We hear her, and we see with her eyes; we go from the grass-turf house up to the town, to the other grass-turf houses, where poor women sit and make lace, once the celebrated work of the rich nuns here in the cloister's wealthy time.

How still, solitary and grass-grown are these streets! We stop by an old wall, mouldy-green for centuries already. Within it stood the cloister; now there is but one of its wings remaining. There, within that now poor garden still bloom Saint Bridget's leek, and once ran flowers. King John and the Abbess, Ana Gylte, wandered one evening there, and the King cunningly asked: "If the maidens in the cloister were never tempted by love?" and the Abbess answered, as she pointed to a bird that just then flew over them: "It may happen! One cannot prevent the bird from flying over the garden; but one may surely prevent it from building its nest there!"

Thus thought the pious Abbess, and there have been sisters who thought and acted like her. But it is quite as sure that in the same garden there stood a pear-tree, called the tree of death; and the legend says of it, that whoever approached and plucked its fruit would soon die. Red and yellow pears weighed down its branches to the ground. The trunk was unusually large; the grass grew high around it, and many a morning hour was it seen trodden down. Who had been here during the night?

A storm arose one evening from the lake, and the next morning the large tree was found thrown down; the trunk was broken, and out from it there rolled infants' bones—the white bones of murdered children lay shining in the grass.

The pious but love-sick sister Ingrid, this Vadstene's Heloise, writes to her heart's beloved, Axel Nilsun—for the chronicles have preserved it for us:—

"Broderne og Systarne leka paa Spil, drikke Vin och dansa med hvarandra i Tradgarden!"

(The brothers and sisters amuse themselves in play, drink wine and dance with one another in the garden).

These words may explain to us the history of the pear-tree: one is led to think of the orgies of the nun-phantoms in "Robert le Diable," the daughters of sin on consecrated ground. But "judge not, lest ye be judged," said the purest and best of men that was born of woman. We will read Sister Ingrid's letter, sent secretly to him she truly loved. In it lies the history of many, clear and human to us:—

"Jag djerfues for ingen utan for dig allena bekaenna, att jag formar ilia anda mit Ave Maria eller laesa mit Paternoster, utan du kommer mig ichagen. Ja i sjelfa messen kommer mig fore dit taeckleliga Ansigte och vart karliga omgange. Jag tycker jag kan icke skifta mig for n genann an Menniska, jungfru Maria, St. Birgitta och himmelens Haerskaror skalla kanske straffe mig harfar? Men du vet det val, hjertans kaeraste att jag med fri vilja och uppsaet aldrig dissa reglar samtykt. Mine foraeldrer hafva vael min kropp i dette fangelset insatt, men hjertaet kan intet sa snart fran verlden ater kalles!"

(I dare not confess to any other than to thee, that I am not able to repeat my Ave Maria or read my Paternoster, without calling thee to mind. Nay, even in the mass itself thy comely face appears, and our affectionate intercourse recurs to me. It seems to me that I cannot confess to any other human being—the Virgin Mary, St. Bridget, and the whole host of heaven will perhaps punish me for it. But thou knowest well, my heart's beloved, that I have never consented with my free-will to these rules. My parents, it is true, have placed my body in this prison, but the heart cannot so soon be weaned from the world).

How touching is the distress of young hearts! It offers itself to us from the mouldy parchment, it resounds in old songs. Beg the grey-haired old dame in the grass turf-house to sing to thee of the young, heavy sorrow, of the saving angel—and the angel came in many shapes. You will hear the song of the cloister robbery; of Herr Carl who was sick to death; when the young nun entered the corpse chamber, sat down by his feet and whispered how sincerely she had loved him, and the knight rose from his bier and bore her away to marriage and pleasure in Copenhagen. And all the nuns of the cloister sang: "Christ grant that such an angel were to come, and take both me and thee!"

The old dame will also sing for thee of the beautiful Ogda and Oluf Tyste; and at once the cloister is revived in its splendour, the bells ring, stone houses arise—they even rise from the waters of the Vettern: the little town becomes churches and towers. The streets are crowded with great, with sober, well-dressed persons. Down the stairs of the town hall descends with a sword by his side and in fur-lined cloak, the most wealthy citizen of Vadstene, the merchant Michael. By his side is his young, beautiful daughter Agda, richly-dressed and happy; youth in beauty, youth in mind. All eyes are turned on the rich man—and yet forget him for her, the beautiful. Life's best blessings await her; her thoughts soar upwards, her mind aspires; her future is happiness! These were the thoughts of the many—and amongst the many there was one who saw her as Romeo saw Juliet, as Adam saw Eve in the garden of Paradise. That one was Oluf, the handsomest young man, but poor as Agda was rich. And he must conceal his love; but as only he lived in it, only he knew of it; so he became mute and still, and after months had passed away, the town's folk called him Oluf Tyste (Oluf the silent).

Nights and days he combated his love; nights and days he suffered inexpressible torment; but at last—one dew-drop or one sunbeam alone is necessary for the ripe rose to open its leaves—he must tell it to Agda. And she listened to his words, was terrified, and sprang away; but the thought remained with him, and the heart went after the thought and stayed there; she returned his love strongly and truly, but in modesty and honour; and therefore poor Oluf came to the rich merchant and sought his daughter's hand. But Michael shut the bolts of his door and his heart too. He would neither listen to tears nor supplications, but only to his own will; and as little Agda also kept firm to her will, her father placed her in Vadstene cloister. And Oluf was obliged to submit, as it is recorded in the old song, that they cast

> "—*den svarta Muld*
> *Alt oefver skoen Agdas arm.*" [b]

She was dead to him and the world. But one night, in tempestuous weather, whilst the rain streamed down, Oluf Tyste came to the cloister wall, threw his rope-ladder over it, and however high the Vettern lifted its waves, Oluf and little Agda flew away over its fathomless depths that autumn night.

Early in the morning the nuns missed little Agda. What a screaming and shouting—the cloister is disgraced! The Abbess and Michael the merchant swore that vengeance and death should reach the fugitives. Lindkjoeping's severe bishop, Hans Brask, fulminated his ban over them, but they were already across the waters of the Vettern; they had reached the shores of the Venern, they were on Kinnakulla, with one of Oluf's friends, who owned the delightful Hellekis.

Here their marriage was to be celebrated. The guests were invited, and a monk from the neighbouring cloister of Husaby, was fetched to marry them. Then came the messenger with the bishop's excommunication, and this—but not the marriage ceremony—was read to them.

All turned away from them terrified. The owner of the house, the friend of Oluf's youth, pointed to the open door and bade them depart instantly. Oluf only requested a car and horse wherewith to convey away his exhausted Agda; but they threw sticks and stones after them, and Oluf was obliged to bear his poor bride in his arms far into the forest.

Heavy and bitter was their wandering. At last, however, they found a home: it was in Guldkroken, in West Gothland. An honest old couple gave them shelter and a place by the hearth: they stayed there till Christmas, and on that holy eve there was to be a real Christmas festival. The guests were invited, the furmenty set forth; and now came the clergyman of the parish to

---

b   The black mould over the beautiful Agda's arm.

say prayers; but whilst he spoke he recognised Oluf and Agda, and the prayer became a curse upon the two. Anxiety and terror came over all; they drove the excommunicated pair out of the house, out into the biting frost, where the wolves went in flocks, and the bear was no stranger. And Oluf felled wood in the forest, and kindled a fire to frighten away the noxious animals and keep life in Agda—he thought that she must die. But just then she was stronger of the two.

"Our Lord is almighty and gracious; He will not leave us!" said she. "He has one here on the earth, one who can save us, one, who has proved like us, what it is to wander amongst enemies and wild animals. It is the King—Gustavus Vasa! He has languished like us!—gone astray in Dalecarlia in the deep snow! he has suffered, tried, knows it—he can and he will help us!"

The King was in Vadstene. He had called together the representatives of the kingdom there. He dwelt in the cloister itself, even there where little Agda, if the King did not grant her pardon, must suffer what the angry Abbess dared to advise: penance and a painful death awaited her.

Through forests and by untrodden paths, in storm and snow, Oluf and Agda came to Vadstene. They were seen: some showed fear, others insulted and threatened them. The guard of the cloister made the sign of the cross on seeing the two sinners, who dared to ask admission to the King.

"I will receive and hear all," was his royal message, and the two lovers fell trembling at his feet.

And the King looked mildly on them; and as he long had had the intention to humiliate the proud Bishop of Lindkjoeping, the moment was not unfavourable to them; the King listened to the relation of their lives and sufferings, and gave them his word, that the excommunication should be annulled. He then placed their hands one in the other, and said that the priest should also do the same soon; and he promised them his royal protection and favour.

And old Michael, the merchant, who feared the King's anger, with which he was threatened, became so mild and gentle, that he, as the King commanded, not only opened his house and his arms to Oluf and Agda, but displayed all his riches on the wedding-day of the young couple. The marriage ceremony took place in the cloister church, whither the King himself led the bride, and where, by his command, all the nuns were obliged to be present, in order to give still more ecclesiastical pomp to the festival. And many a heart there silently recalled the old song about the cloister robbery and looked at Oluf Tyste:

"Krist gif en sadan Angel
Kom, tog bad mig och dig!"[c]

The sun now shines through the open cloister-gate. Let truth shine into our hearts; let us likewise acknowledge the cloister's share of God's influence. Every cell was not quite a prison, where the imprisoned bird flew in despair against the window-pane; here sometimes was sunshine from God in the heart and mind, from hence also went out comfort and blessings. If the dead could rise from their graves they would bear witness thereof: if we saw them in the moonlight lift the tombstone and step forth towards the cloister, they would say: "Blessed be these walls!" if we saw them in the sunlight hovering in the rainbow's gleam, they would say: "Blessed be these walls!"

How changed the rich, mighty Vadstene cloister, where the first daughters of the land were nuns, where the young nobles of the land wore the monk's cowl. Hither they made pilgrimages from Italy, from Spain: from far distant lands, in snow and cold, the pilgrim came barefooted to the cloister door. Pious men and women bore the corpse of St. Bridget hither in their hands from Rome, and all the church-bells in all the lands and towns they passed through, tolled when they came.

We go towards the cloister—the remains of the old ruin. We enter St. Bridget's cell—it still stands unchanged. It is low, small and narrow: four diminutive frames form the whole window, but one can look from it out over the whole garden, and far away over the Vettern. We see the same beautiful landscape that the fair Saint saw as a frame around her God, whilst she read her morning and evening prayers. In the tile-stone of the floor there is engraved a rosary: before it, on her bare knees, she said a pater-noster at every pearl there pointed out. Here is no chimney—no hearth, no place for it. Cold and solitary it is, and was, here where the world's most far-famed woman dwelt, she who by her own sagacity, and by her contemporaries was raised to the throne of female saints.

---

c Christ grant that such an angel were to come, and take both me and thee!

From this poor cell we enter one still meaner, one still more narrow and cold, where the faint light of day struggles in through a long crevice in the wall. Glass there never was here: the wind blows in here. Who was she who once dwelt in this cell?

In our times they have arranged light, warm chambers close by: a whole range opens into the broad passage. We hear merry songs; laughter we hear, and weeping: strange figures nod to us from these chambers. Who are these? The rich cloister of St. Bridget's, whence kings made pilgrimages, is now Sweden's madhouse. And here the numerous travellers write their names on the wall. We hasten from the hideous scene into the splendid cloister church,—the blue church, as it is called, from the blue stones of which the walls are built—and here, where the large stones of the floor cover great men, abbesses and queens, only one monument is noticeable, that of a knightly figure carved in stone, which stands aloft before the altar. It is that of the insane Duke Magnus. Is it not as if he stepped forth from amongst the dead, and announced that such afflicted creatures were to be where St. Bridget once ruled?

Pace lightly over the floor! Thy foot treads on the graves of the pious: the flat, modest stone here in the corner covers the dust of the noble Queen Philippa. She, that mighty England's daughter, the great-hearted, the immortal woman, who with wisdom and courage defended her consort's throne, that consort who rudely and barbarously cast her off! Vadstene's cloister gave her shelter—the grave here gave her rest.

We seek one grave. It is not known—it is forgotten, as she was in her lifetime. Who was she? The cloistered sister Elizabeth, daughter of the Holstein Count, and once the bride of King Hakon of Norway. Sweet creature! she proudly—but not with unbecoming pride—advanced in her bridal dress, and with her court ladies, up to her royal consort. Then came King Valdemar, who by force and fraud stopped the voyage, and induced Hakon to marry Margaret, then eleven years of age, who thereby got the crown of Norway. Elizabeth was sent to Vadstene cloister, where her will was not asked. Afterwards when Margaret—who justly occupies a great place in the history of Scandinavia, but only comparatively a small one in the hearts—sat on the throne, powerful and respected, visited the then flourishing Vadstene, where the Abbess of the cloister was St. Bridget's grand-daughter, her childhood's friend, Margaret kissed every monk on the cheek. The legend is well known about him, the handsomest, who thereupon blushed. She kissed every nun on the hand, and also Elizabeth, her, whom she would only see here. Whose heart throbbed loudest at that kiss? Poor Elizabeth, thy grave is forgotten, but not the wrong thou didst suffer.

We now enter the sacristy. Here, under a double coffin lid, rests an age's holiest saint in the North, Vadstene cloister's diadem and lustre—St. Bridget.

On the night she was born, says the legend, there appeared a beaming cloud in the heavens, and on it stood a majestic virgin, who said: "Of Birger is born a daughter whose admirable voice shall be heard over the whole world." This delicate and singular child grew up in the castle of her father, Knight Brake. Visions and revelations appeared to her, and these increased when she, only thirteen years of age, was married to the rich Ulf Gudmundsen, and became the mother of many children. "Thou shalt be my bride and my agent," she heard Christ say, and every one of her actions was, as she averred, according to his announcement. After this she went to Niddaros, to St. Oluf's holy shrine: she then went to Germany, France, Spain and Rome.

Sometimes honoured and sometimes mocked, she travelled, even to Cyprus and Palestine. Conscious of approaching death, she again reached Rome, where her last revelation was, that she should rest in Vadstene, and that this cloister especially should be sanctified by God's love. The splendour of the Northern lights does not extend so far around the earth as the glory of this fair saint, who now is but a legend. We bend with silent, serious thoughts before the mouldering remains in the coffin here—those of St. Bridget and her daughter St. Catherine; but even of these the remembrance will be extinguished. There is a tradition amongst the people, that in the time of the Reformation the real remains were carried off to a cloister in Poland, but this is not certainly known. Vadstene, at least, is not the repository of St. Bridget and her daughter's dust.

Vadstene was once great and glorious. Great was the cloister's power, as St. Bridget saw it in the prospect of death. Where is now the cloister's might? It reposes under the tomb-stones—the graves alone speak of it. Here, under our feet, only a few steps from the church door, is a stone in which are carved fourteen rings: they announce that fourteen farms were given to the cloister, in order that he who moulders here might have this place, fourteen feet within the church door. It was Boa Johnson Grip, a great sinner; but the cloister's power was greater than that of all sinners: the stone on his grave records it with no ordinary significance of language.

Gustavus, the first Vasa, was the sun—the ruling power: the brightness of the cloister star must needs pale before him.

There yet stands a stone outline of Vadstene's rich palace which he erected, with towers and spires, close by the cloister. At a far distance on the Vettern, it looks as if it still stood in all its splendour; near, in moonlight nights, it appears the same unchanged edifice, for the fathom-thick walls yet remain; the carvings over the windows and gates stand forth in light and shade, and the moat round about, which is only separated from the Vettern by the narrow carriage road, takes the reflection of the immense building as a mirrored image.

We now stand before it in daylight. Not a pane of glass is to be found in it; planks and old doors are nailed fast to the window frames; the balls alone still stand on the two towers, broad, heavy, and resembling colossal toadstools. The iron spire of the one still towers aloft in the air; the other spire is bent: like the hands on a sundial it shows the time—the time that is gone. The other two balls are half fallen down; lambs frisk about between the beams, and the space below is used as a cow-stall.

The arms over the gateway have neither spot nor blemish: they seem as if carved yesterday; the walls are firm, and the stairs look like new. In the palace yard, far above the gateway, the great folding door was opened, whence once the minstrels stepped out and played a welcome greeting from the balcony, but even this is broken down: we go through the spacious kitchen, from whose white walls, a sketch of Vadstene palace, ships, and flowering trees, in red chalk, still attract the eye.

Here where they cooked and roasted, is now a large empty space: even the chimney is gone; and from the ceiling where thick, heavy beams of timber have been placed close to one another, there hangs the dust-covered cobweb, as if the whole were a mass of dark grey dropping stones.

We walk from hall to hall, and the wooden shutters are opened to admit daylight. All is vast, lofty, spacious, and adorned with antique chimney-pieces, and from every window there is a charming prospect over the clear, deep Vettern. In one of the chambers in the ground floor sat the insane Duke Magnus, (whose stone image we lately saw conspicuous in the church) horrified at having signed his own brother's death-warrant; dreamingly in love with the portrait of Scotland's Queen, Mary Stuart; paying court to her and expecting to see the ship, with her, glide over the sea towards Vadstene. And she came—he thought she came—in the form of a mermaid, raising herself aloft on the water: she nodded and called to him, and the unfortunate Duke sprang out of the window down to her. We gazed out of this window, and below it we saw the deep moat in which he sank.

We enter the yeoman's hall, and the council hall, where, in the recesses of the windows, on each side, are painted yeomen in strange dresses, half Dalecarlians and half Roman warriors.

In this once rich saloon, Svanta Steenson Sture knelt to Sweden's Queen, Catherine Lejonhufved: she was Svanta Sture's love, before Gustavus Vasa's will made her his Queen. The lovers met here: the walls are silent as to what they said, when the door was opened and the King entered, and saw the kneeling Sture, and asked what it meant. Margaret answered craftily and hastily: "He demands my sister Martha's hand in marriage!" and the King gave Svanta Sture the bride the Queen had asked for him.

We are now in the royal bridal chamber, whither King Gustavus led his third consort. Catherine Steenbock, also another's bride, the bride of the Knight Gustavus. It is a sad story.

Gustavus of the three roses, was in his youth honoured by the King, who sent him on a mission to the Emperor Charles the Fifth. He returned adorned with the Emperor's costly golden chain—young, handsome, joyous and richly clad, he returned home, and knew well how to relate the magnificence and charms of foreign lands: young and old listened to him with admiration, but young Catherine most of all. Through him the world in her eyes became twice as large, rich, and beautiful; they became dear to each other, and their parents blessed their love. The love-pledge was to be drunk,—when there came a message from the King, that the young Knight must, without delay, again bear a letter and greeting to the Emperor Charles. The betrothed pair separated with heavy hearts, but with a promise of mutual inviolable troth. The King then invited Catherine's parents to come to Vadstene palace. Catherine was obliged to accompany them; here King Gustavus saw her for the first time, and the old man fell in love with her.

Christmas was kept with great hilarity; there were song and harp in these halls, and the King himself played the lute. When the time came for departure, the King said to Catherine's mother, that he would marry the young girl.

"But she is the bride of the Knight Gustavus!" stammered the mother.

"Young hearts soon forget their sorrows," thought the King. The mother thought so likewise, and as there chanced to come a letter the same day and hour from the young Knight Gustavus, Fra Steenbock committed it to the flames. All the letters that came afterwards and all the letters that Catherine wrote, were burnt by her mother, and doubts and evil reports were whispered to Catherine, that she was forgotten abroad by her young lover. But Catherine was secure and firm in her belief of him. In the spring her parents made known to her the King's proposal, and praised her good fortune. She answered seriously and determinedly, "No!" and when they repeated to her that it should and must happen, she repeatedly screamed in the greatest anguish, "No no!" and sank exhausted at her father and mother's feet, and humbly prayed them not to force her.

And the mother wrote to the King that all was going on well, but that her child was bashful. The King now announced his visit to Torpe, where her parents, the Steenbocks, dwelt. The King was received with rejoicing and feasting, but Catherine had disappeared and the King himself was the successful one who found her. She sat dissolved in tears under the wild rose tree, where she had bidden farewell to her heart's beloved.

There was merry song and joyous life in the old mansion; Catherine alone was sorrowful and silent. Her mother had brought her all her jewels and ornaments, but she wore none of them: she had put on her simplest dress, but in this she only fascinated the old King the more, and he would have that their betrothal should take place before he departed. Fra Steenbock wrested the Knight Gustavus's ring from Catherine's finger, and whispered in her ear:

"It will cost the friend of thy youth his life and fortune; the King can do everything!" And the parents led her to King Gustavus, showed him that the ring was from the maiden's hand; and the King placed his own golden ring on her finger in the other's stead. In the month of August the flag waved from the mast of the royal yacht which bore the young Queen over the Vettern. Princes and knights, in costly robes, stood by the shore, music played, and the people shouted. Catherine made her entry into Vadstene Palace. The nuptials were celebrated the following day, and the walls were hung with silk and velvet, with cloth of gold and silver! It was a festival and rejoicing. Poor Catherine!

In November, the Knight Gustavus of the three roses, returned home. His prudent, noble mother, Christina Gyldenstjerne, met him at the frontiers of the kingdom, prepared him, consoled him, and soothed his mind: she accompanied him by slow stages to Vadstene, where they were both invited by the King to remain during the Christmas festival. They accepted the invitation, but the Knight Gustavus was not to be moved to come to the King's table or any other place where the Queen was to be found. The Christmas approached. One Sunday evening, Gustavus was disconsolate; the Knight was long sleepless, and at daybreak he went into the church, to the tomb of his ancestress, St. Bridget. There he saw, at a few paces from him, a female kneeling before Philippa's tomb. It was the Queen he saw; their eyes met, and Gustavus hastened away. She then mentioned his name, begged him to stay, and commanded him to do so.

"I command it, Gustavus!" said she; "the Queen commands it."

And she spoke to him; they conversed together, and it became clear to them both what had been done against them and with them; and she showed him a withered rose which she kept in her bosom, and she bent towards him and gave him a kiss, the last—their eternal leave-taking—and then they separated. He died shortly afterwards, but Catherine was stronger, yet not strong enough for her heart's deep sorrow. Here, in the bed-chamber, in uneasy dreams, says the story, she betrayed in sleep the constant thought of her heart, her youth's love, to the King, saying: "Gustavus I love dearly; but the rose—I shall never forget."

From a secret door we walk out on to the open rampart, where the sheep now graze; the cattle are driven into one of the ruined towers. We see the palace-yard, and look from it up to a window. Come, thou birch-wood's thrush, and warble thy lays; sing, whilst we recal the bitterness of love in the rude—the chivalrous ages.

Under that window there stood, one cold winter's night, wrapped in his white cloak, the young Count John of East Friesland. His brother had married Gustavus Vasa's eldest daughter, and departed with her to his home: wherever they came on their journey, there was mirth and feasting, but the most splendid was at Vadstene Palace. Cecilia, the King's younger daughter, had accompanied her sister hither, and was here, as everywhere, the first, the most beautiful in the chase as well as at the tournament. The winter began directly on their arrival at Vadstene; the cold was severe, and the Vettern frozen over. One day, Cecilia rode out on the ice and it broke; her brother, Prince Erik, came galloping to her aid. John, of East Friesland, was already there, and begged Erik to dismount, as he would, being on horseback, break the ice still more. Erik would not listen to him, and as John saw that there was no time for dispute, he dragged Erik from the horse, sprang into the water himself, and saved Cecilia. Prince Erik was furious with wrath, and no one could appease him. Cecilia lay long in a fever, and during its continuance, her love for him who had saved her life increased. She recovered, and they understood each other, but the day of separation approached. It was on the night previous that John, in his white cloak, ascended from stone to stone, holding by his silk ladder, until he at length entered the window; here they would converse for hours in all modesty and honour, speak about his return and their nuptials the following year; and whilst they sat there the door was hewn down with axes. Prince Erik entered, and raised the murderous weapon to slay the young Lord of East Friesland, when Cecilia threw herself between them. But Erik commanded his menials to seize the lover, whom they put in irons and cast into a low, dark hole, that cold frosty night, and the next day, without even giving him a morsel of bread or a drop of water, he was thrown on to a peasant's sledge, and dragged before the King to receive judgment. Erik himself cast his sister's fair name and fame into slander's babbling pool, and high dames and citizens' wives washed unspotted innocence in calumny's impure waters.

It is only when the large wooden shutters of the saloons are opened, that the sunbeams stray in here; the dust accumulates in their twisted pillars, and is only just disturbed by the draught of air. In here is a warehouse for corn. Great fat rats make their nests in these halls. The spider spins mourning banners under the beams. This is Vadstene Palace!

We are filled with sad thoughts. We turn our eyes from this place towards the lowly house with the grass-turf roof, where the little lamb crops the grass under the cherry-tree, which strews its fragrant leaves over it. Our thoughts descend from the rich cloister, from the proud palace, to the grassy turf, and the sun fades away over the grassy turf, and the old dame goes to sleep under the grassy turf, below which lie the mighty memorials of Vadstene.

THE PUPPET-SHOWMAN

There was an elderly man on the steam-boat, with such a contented face that, if it did not lie, he must be the happiest man on earth. That he indeed said he was: I heard it from his own mouth. He was a Dane, consequently my countryman, and was a travelling theatrical manager. He had the whole *corps dramatique* with him; they lay in a large chest—he was a puppet showman. His innate good-humour, said he, had been tried by a polytechnic candidate,[d] and from this experiment on his patience he had become completely happy. I did not understand him at the moment, but he soon laid the whole case clearly before me; and here it is.

"It was in Slagelse," said he, "that I gave a representation at the parsonage, and had a brilliant house and a brilliant company of spectators, all young persons, unconfirmed, except a few old ladies. Then there came a person dressed in black, having the appearance of a student: he sat down amongst the others, laughed quite at the proper time, and applauded quite correctly; that was an unusual spectator!

"I was bent on ascertaining who he was, and then I heard that he was a candidate from the polytechnic school, who had been sent out to instruct people in the provinces. At eight o'clock my representation was over; the children were to go early to bed, and one must think of the convenience of the public.

"At nine o'clock the candidate began his lectures and experiments, and now *I* was one of *his* auditory.

---

d   One who has passed his examination at a polytechnic school.

"It was remarkable to hear and look at! The chief part of it went over my head and into the parson's, as one says. Can it be possible, thought I, that we human beings can find out such things? in that case, we must also be able to hold out longer, before we are put into the earth. It was merely small miracles that he performed, and yet all as easy as an old stocking—quite from nature. In the time of Moses and the prophets, such a polytechnic candidate would have been one of the wise men of the land, and in the Middle Ages he would have been burnt. I could not sleep the whole night, and as I gave a representation the next evening, and the candidate was there again, I got into a real merry humour.

"I have heard of an actor, who when playing the lovers' parts, only thought of one of the spectators; he played for *her* alone, and forgot all the rest of the house; the polytechnic candidate was my *her*, my only spectator, for whom I played. And when the performance was over, all the puppets were called forward, and I was invited by the polytechnic candidate to take a glass of wine with him; and he spoke about my comedy, and I of his science; and I believe we each derived equal pleasure from the other. But yet I had the advantage, for there was so much in his performance that he could not account for: as for instance, that a piece of iron which falls through a spiral line, becomes magnetic,—well, how is that? The spirit comes over it, but whence does it come from? it is just as with the human beings of this world, I think; our Lord lets them fall through the spiral line of time, and the spirit comes over them—and there stands a Napoleon, a Luther, or a similar person.

"'All nature is a series of miracles,' said the candidate, 'but we are so accustomed to them that we call them things of every-day life.' And he spoke and he explained, so that it seemed at last as if he lifted my scull, and I honestly confessed, that if I were not an old fellow, I would go directly to the polytechnic school, and learn to examine the world in the summer, although I was one of the happiest of men.

"'One of the happiest!' said he, and it was just as if he tasted it. 'Are you happy?' 'Yes!' said I, 'I am happy, and I am welcome in all the towns I come to with my company! There is certainly one wish, that comes now and then like a night-mare, which rides on my good-humour, and that is to be a theatrical manager for a living company—a company of real men and women.'

"'You wish to have your puppets animated; you would have them become real actors and actresses,' said he, 'and yourself be the manager? you then think that you would be perfectly happy?'

"Now he did not think so, but I thought so; and we talked for and against; and we were just as near in our opinions as before. But we clinked our glasses together, and the wine was very good; but there was witchcraft in it, or else the short and the long of the story would be—that I was intoxicated.

"That I was not; my eyes were quite clear; it was as if there was sunshine in the room, and it shone out of the face of the polytechnic candidate, so that I began to think of the old gods in my youth, and when they went about in the world. And I told him so, and then he smiled, and I durst have sworn that he was a disguised god, or one of the family!—And he was so—my first wish was to be fulfilled: the puppets become living beings and I the manager of men and women. We drank that it should be so! he put all my puppets in the wooden chest, fastened it on my back, and then let me fall through a spiral line. I can still hear how I came down, slap! I lay on the floor, that is quite sure and certain, and the whole company sprang out of the chest. The spirit had come over us all together; all the puppets had become excellent artists—they said so themselves—and I was the manager. Everything was in order for the first representation; the whole company must speak with me, and the public also. The female dancer said, that if she did not stand on one leg, the house would be in an uproar: she was master of the whole and would be treated as such.

"She who played the queen, would also be treated as a queen when off the stage, or else she should get out of practice, and he who was employed to come in with a letter made himself as important as the first lover. 'For,' said he, 'the small are of just as much importance as the great, in an artistic whole.' Then the hero demanded that the whole of his part should only be retorts on making his exit, for these the public applauded; the prima donna would only play in a red light, for that suited her best—she would not be blue: they were all like flies in a bottle, and I was also in the bottle—for I was the manager. I lost my breath, my head was quite dizzy! I was as miserable as a man can be; it was a new race of beings I had come amongst; I wished that I had them altogether again in the chest, that I had never been a manager: I told them that they were in fact only puppets, and so they beat me to death. That was my feeling!

"I lay on the bed in my chamber; but how I had come there from the polytechnic candidate, he must know best—for I do not. The moon shone in on the floor where the puppet-chest lay upset, and all the puppets spread about—great and small, the whole lot. But I was not floored! I sprang out of bed, and threw them all into the chest; some on their heads, and some on their legs; I smacked the lid down and sat myself upon it: it was worth painting, can't you conceive it? I can! 'Now you shall be there!' said I, 'and I will never more wish that you may become flesh and blood!' I was so glad; I was the happiest man alive—the polytechnic candidate had tried me! I sat in perfect bliss, and fell asleep on the chest; and in the morning—it was, properly speaking, at noon, for I slept so very long that morning—I sat there still, happy and edified—I saw that my previous and only wish had been stupid. I inquired for the polytechnic candidate, but he was gone, like the Greek and Roman gods.

"And from that time I have been the happiest man alive. I am a fortunate manager; my company does not argue with me, neither does the public; they are amused to their heart's content, and I can myself put all my pieces nicely together. I take the best parts out of all sorts of comedies that I choose, and no one troubles himself about it. Pieces that are now despised at the large theatres, but which thirty years ago the public ran to see, and cried over—those pieces I now make use of. I now present them before the young folks; and the young folks—they cry just as their fathers and mothers used to do. I give 'Johanna Montfakon' and 'Dyveke,' but abbreviated; for the little folks do not like long, twaddling love-stories. They must have it unfortunate—but it must be brief. Now that I have travelled through Denmark, both to the right and left, I know everybody and am known again. Now I have come to Sweden, and if I am successful and gain much money, I will be a Scandinavian, if the humour hold; and this I tell you, as you are my countryman."

And I, as his countryman, naturally tell it again—only for the sake of telling it.

THE "SKJAERGAARDS"

✦

The canal voyage through Sweden goes at first constantly up-wards, through elvs and lakes, forests and rocky land. From the heights we look down on vast extents of forest-land and large waters, and by degrees the vessel sinks again down through mountain torrents. At Mem we are again down by the salt fiord: a solitary tower raises its head between the remains of low, thick walls—it is the ruins of Stegeberg. The coast is covered to a great extent with dark, melancholy forests, which enclose small grass-grown valleys. The screaming sea-gulls fly around our vessel; we are by the Baltic; we feel the fresh sea-breeze: it blows as in the times of the ancient heroes, when the sea-kings, sons of high-born fathers, exercised their deeds here. The same sea's surface then appeared to them as now to us, with its numberless isles, which lie strewed about here in the water by thousands along the whole coast. The depth of water between the rocky isles and the solid land is that we call "The Skjaergaards:" their waters flow into each other with varying splendour. We see it in the sunshine, and it is like a large English landscape garden; but the greensward plain is here the deep sea, the flower-beds in it are rocks and reefs, rich in firs and pines, oaks and bushes. Mark how, when the wind blows from the east, and the sea breaks over sunken rocks and is dashed back again in spray from the cliffs, your limbs feel—even through the ship on which you stand—the power of the sea: you are lifted as if by supernatural hands.

We rush on against wind and sea, as if it were the sea-god's snorting horse that bore us; from Skjaergaard to Skjaergaard. The signal-gun is fired, and the pilot comes from that solitary wooden house. Sometimes we look upon the open sea, sometimes we glide again in between dark, stony islands; they lie like gigantic monsters in the water: one has the form of the tortoise's arched shell, another has the elephant's back and rough grey colour. Mouldering, light grey rocks indicate that the wind and weather past centuries has lashed over them.

We now approach larger rocky islands, and the huge, grey, broken rocks of the main land, where dwarfish pine woods grow in a continual combat with the blast; the Skjaergaards sometimes become only a narrow canal, sometimes an extensive lake strewed with small islets, all of stone, and often only a mere block of stone, to which a single little fir-tree clings fast: screaming sea-gulls flutter around the land-marks that are set up; and now we see a single farm-house, whose red-painted sides shine forth from the dark background. A group of cows lies basking in the sun on the stony surface, near a little smiling pasture, which appears to have been cultivated here or cut out of a meadow in Scania. How solitary must it not be to live on that little island! Ask the boy who sits there by the cattle, he will be able to tell us. "It is lively and merry here," says he. "The day is so long and light, the seal sits out there on the stone and barks in the early morning hour, and all the steamers from the canal must pass here. I know them all; and when the sun goes down in the evening, it is a whole history to look into the clouds over the land: there stand mountains with palaces, in silver and in gold, in red and in blue; sailing dragons with golden crowns, or an old giant with a beard down to his waist—altogether of clouds, and they are always changing.

"The storms come on in the autumn, and then there is often much anxiety when father is out to help ships in distress; but one becomes, as it were, a new being.

"In winter the ice is locked fast and firm, and we drive from island to island and to the main land; and if the bear or the wolf pays us a visit we take his skin for a winter covering: it is warm in the room there, and they read and tell stories about old times!"

Yes, old Time, how thou dost unfold thyself with remembrances of these very Skjaergaards—old Time which belonged to the brave. These waters, these rocky isles and strands, saw heroes more greatly active than actively good: they swung the axe to give the mortal blow, or as they called it, "the whining Jetteqvinde." [e]

Here came the Vikings with their ships: on the headland yonder they levied provisions; the grazing cattle were slaughtered and borne away. Ye mouldering cliffs, had ye but a tongue, ye might tell us about the duels with the two-handed sword—about the deeds of the giants. Ye saw the hero hew with the sword, and cast the javelin: his left hand was as cunning as his right The sword moved so quickly in the air that there seemed to be three. Ye saw him, when he in all his martial array sprang forwards and backwards, higher than he himself was tall, and if he sprang into the sea he swam like a whale. Ye saw the two combatants: the one darted his javelin, the other caught it in the air, and cast it back again, so that it pierced through shield and man down into the earth. Ye saw warriors with sharp swords and angry hearts; the sword was struck downwards so as to cut the knee, out the combatant sprang into the air, and the sword whizzed under his feet. Mighty Sagas from the olden times! Mouldering rocks, could ye but tell us of these things!

Ye, deep waters, bore the Vikings' ships, and when the strong in battle lifted the iron anchor and cast it against the enemy's vessel, so that the planks were rent asunder, ye poured your dark heavy seas into the hold, so that the bark sank. The wild *Berserk* who with naked breast stood against his enemy's blows, mad as a dog, howling like a bear, tearing his shield asunder, rushing to the bottom of the sea here, and fetching up stones, which ordinary men could not raise—history peoples these waters, these cliffs for us! A future poet will conjure them to this Scandinavian Archipelago, chisel the true forms out of the old Sagas, the bold, the rude, the greatness and imperfections of the time, in their habits as they lived.

They rise again for us on yonder island, where the wind is whistling through the young fir wood. The house is of beams, roofed with bark; the smoke from the fire on the broad stone in the hall, whirls through the air-hole, near which stands the cask of mead; the cushions lie on the bench before the closed bedsteads; deer-skins hang over the balk walls, ornamented with shields, helmets, and armour. Effigies of gods, carved, on wooden poles, stand before the high seat where the noble Viking sits, a high-born father's youngest son, great in fame, but still greater in deeds; the skjalds (bards) and

---

e   Giantess.

foster-brothers sit nearest to him. They defended the coasts of their countrymen, and the pious women; they fetched wheat and honey from England, they went to the White Sea for sables and furs—their adventures are related in song. We see the old man ride in rich clothing, with gloves sewn with golden thread, and with a hat brought from Garderige; we see the youth with a golden fillet around his brow; we see him at the *Thing;* we see him in battle and in play, where the best is he that can cut off the other's eyebrows without scratching the skin, or causing a wink with the eyes, on pain of losing his station. The woman sits in the log-house at her loom, and in the late moonlight nights the spirits of the fallen come and sit down around the fire, where they shake the wet, dripping clothes; but the serf sleeps in the ashes, and on the kitchen bench, and dreams that he dips his bread in the fat soup, and licks his fingers.

Thou future poet, thou wilt call forth the vanished forms from the Sagas, thou wilt people these islands, and let us glide past these reminiscences of the olden time with the mind full of them; clearly and truly wilt thou let us glide, as we now with the power of steam fly past that firmly standing scenery, the swelling sea, rocks and reefs, the main land, and wood-grown islands.

We are already past Braavigen, where numberless ships from the northern kingdoms lay, when Upsala's King, Sigurd Ring, came, challenged by Harald Hildetand, who, old and grey, feared to die on a sick bed, and would fall in battle; and the mainland thundered like the plains of Marathon beneath the tramp of horses' hoofs during the battle:[f] bards and female warriors surrounded the Danish King. The blind old man raised himself high in his chariot, gave his horse free rein, and hewed his way. Odin himself had due reverence paid to Hildetand's bones; and the pile was kindled, and the King laid on it, and Sigurd conjured all to cast gold and weapons, the most valuable they possessed, into the fire; and the bards sang to it, and the female warriors struck the spears on the bright shields. Upsala's Lord, Sigurd Ring, became King of Sweden and Denmark: so says the Saga, which sounded over the land and water from these coasts.

The memorials of olden times pass swiftly through our thoughts; we fly past the scene of manly exercises and great deeds in the olden times—the ship cleaves the mighty waters with its iron paddles, from Skjaergaard to Skjaergaard.

---

f   The battle of Braavalla.

STOCKHOLM

We cast runes [g] here on the paper, and from the white ground the picture of Birger Jarl's six hundred years old city rises before thee.

The runes roll, you see! Wood-grown rocky isles appear in the light, grey morning mist; numberless flocks of wild birds build their nests in safety here, where the fresh waters of the Maelaren rush into the salt sea. The Viking's ship comes; King Agna stands by the prow—he brings as booty the King of Finland's daughter. The oak-tree spreads its branches over their bridal chamber; at daybreak the oak-tree bears King Agna, hanged in his long golden chain: that is the bride's work, and the ship sails away again with her and the rescued Fins.

The clouds drive past—the years too.

Hunters and fishermen erect themselves huts;—it is again deserted here, where the sea-birds alone have their homes. What is it that so frightens these numberless flocks? the wild duck and sea-gull fly screaming about, there is a hammering and driving of piles. Oluf Skoetkonge has large beams bored down into the ground, and strong iron chains fastened across the stream: "Thou art caught, Oluf Haraldson,[h] caught with the ships and crews, with which thou didst devastate the royal city Sigtuna; thou canst not escape from the closed Maelar lake!"

---

g   "To cast runes" was, in the olden time, to exercise witchcraft. When the apple, with ciphers cut in it, rolled into the maiden's lap, her heart and mind were infatuated.

h   Afterwards called Saint Oluf.

It is but the work of one night; the same night when Oluf Ha-konson, with iron and with fire, burst his onward way through the stubborn ground; before the day breaks the waters of the Maelar roll there; the Norwegian prince, Oluf sailed through the royal channel he had cut in the east. The stockades, where the iron chains hang, must bear the defences; the citizens from the burnt-down Sigtuna erect themselves a bulwark here, and build their new, little town on stock-holms.[i]

The clouds go, and the years go! Do you see how the gables grow? there rise towers and forts. Birger Jarl makes the town of Stockholm a fortress; the warders stand with bow and arrow on the walls, reconnoitring over lake and fjord, over Brunka-berg sand-ridge. There were the sand-ridge slopes upwards from Roerstrand's Lake they build Clara cloister, and between it and the town a street springs up: several more appear; they form an extensive city, which soon becomes the place of contest for differ-ent partisans, where Ladelaas's sons plant the banner, and where the German Albrecht's retainers burn the Swedes alive within its walls. Stockholm is, however, the heart of the kingdom: that the Danes know well; that the Swedes know too, and there is strife and bloody combating. Blood flows by the executioner's hand, Denmark's Christian the Second, Sweden's executioner, stands in the market-place.

Roll, ye runes! see over Brunkaberg sand-ridge, where the Swedish people conquered the Danish host, there they raise the May-pole: it is midsummer-eve—Gustavus Vasa makes his entry into Stockholm.

Around the May-pole there grow fruit and kitchen-gardens, houses and streets; they vanish in flames, they rise again; that gloomy fortress towards the tower is transformed into a palace, and the city stands magnificently with towers and draw-bridges. There grows a town by itself on the sand-ridge, a third springs up on the rock towards the south; the old walls fall at Gustavus Adolphus's com-mand; the three towns are one, large and extensive, picturesquely varied with old stone houses, wooden shops, and grass-roofed huts; the sun shines on the brass balls of the towers, and a forest of masts stands in that secure harbour.

---

i   Stock, signifies bulks, or beams; holms, i.e. islets, or river islands; hence Stockholm.

Rays of beauty shoot forth into the world from Versailles' painted divinity; they reach the Maelar's strand into Tessin's[j] palace, where art and science are invited as guests with the King, Gustavus the Third, whose effigy cast in bronze is raised on the strand before the splendid palace—it is in our times. The acacia shades the palace's high terrace on whose broad balustrades flowers send forth their perfume from Saxon porcelain; variegated silk curtains hang half-way down before the large glass windows; the floors are polished smooth as a mirror, and under the arch yonder, where the roses grow by the wall, the Endymion of Greece lives eternally in marble. As a guard of honour here, stand Fogelberg's Odin, and Sergei's Amor and Psyche.

We now descend the broad, royal staircase, and before it, where, in by-gone times, Oluf Skoetkonge stretched the iron chains across the mouth of the Maelar Lake, there is now a splendid bridge with shops above and the Streamparterre below: there we see the little steamer 'Nocken,'[k] steering its way, filled with passengers from Diurgarden to the Streamparterre. And what is the Streamparterre? The Neapolitans would tell us: It is in miniature—quite in miniature—the Stockholmers "'Villa Reale." The Hamburgers would say: It is in miniature—quite in miniature—the Stockholmers' "Jungfernstieg."

It is a very little semi-circular island, on which the arches of the bridge rest; a garden full of flowers and trees, which we overlook from the high parapet of the bridge. Ladies and gentlemen promenade there; musicians play, families sit there in groups, and take refreshments in the vaulted halls under the bridge, and look out between the green trees over the open water, to the houses and mansions, and also to the woods and rocks: we forget that we are in the midst of the city.

It is the bridge here that unites Stockholm with Nordmalen, where the greatest part of the fashionable world live, in two long Berlin-like streets; yet amongst all the great houses we will only visit one, and that is the theatre.

We will go on the stage itself—it has an historical signification. Here, by the third side-scene from the stage-lights, to the right, as we look down towards the audience, Gustavus the Third was assas-

---

j   The architect Tessin.
k   The water-sprite.

sinated at a masquerade; and he was borne into that little chamber there, close by the scene, whilst all the outlets were closed, and the motley group of harlequins, polichinellos, wild men, gods and goddesses with unmasked faces, pale and terrified crept together; the dancing ballet-farce had become a real tragedy.

This theatre is Jenny Lind's childhood's home. Here she has sung in the choruses when a little girl; here she first made her appearance in public, and was cheeringly encouraged when a child; here, poor and sorrowful, she has shed tears, when her voice left her, and sent up pious prayers to her Maker. From hence the world's nightingale flew out over distant lands, and proclaimed the purity and holiness of art.

How beautiful it is to look out from the window up here, to look over the water and the Streamparterre to that great, magnificent palace, to Ladegaards land, with the large barracks, to Skipholmen and the rocks that rise straight up from the water, with Soedermalm's gardens, villas, streets, and church cupolas between the green trees: the ships lie there together, so many and so close, with their waving flags. The beautiful, that a poet's eye sees, the world may also see! Roll, ye runes!

There sketches the whole varied prospect; a rainbow extends its arch like a frame around it. Only see! it is sunset, the sky becomes cloudy over Soedermalm, the grey sky becomes darker and darker—a pitch-dark ground—and on it rests a double rainbow. The houses are illumined by so strong a sunlight that the walls seem transparent; the linden-trees in the gardens, which have lately put forth their leaves, appear like fresh, young woods; the long, narrow windows in the Gothic buildings on the island shine as if it were a festal illumination, and between the dark firs there falls a lustre from the panes behind them as of a thousand flames, as if the trees were covered with flickering—Christmas lights; the colours of the rainbow become stronger and stronger, the background darker and darker, and the white sun-lit sea-gulls fly past.

The rainbow has placed one foot high up on Soedermalm's churchyard. Where the rainbow touches the earth, there lie treasures buried, is a popular belief here. The rainbow rests on a grave up there: Stagnalius rests here, Sweden's most gifted singer, so young and so unhappy; and in the same grave lies Nicander, he who sang about King Enzio, and of "Lejonet i Oken;"[1] who sang with a bleeding heart: the fresh vine-leaf cooled the wound and killed the singer. Peace be with his dust—may his songs live for ever! We go to your grave where the rainbow points. The view from here is splendid. The houses rise terrace-like in the steep, paved streets; the foot-passengers can, however, shorten the way by going through narrow lanes, and up steps made of thick beams, and always with a prospect downwards of the water, of the rocks and green trees! It is delightful to dwell here, it is healthy to dwell here, but it is not genteel, as it is by Brunkaberg's sand-ridge, yet it will become so: Stockholm's "Strada Balbi" will one day arise on Soedermalm's rocky ground.

We stand up here. What other city in the world has a better prospect over the salt fjord, over the fresh lake, over towers, cupolas, heaped-up houses, and a palace, which King Enzio himself might have built, and round about the dark, gloomy forests with oaks, pines and firs, so Scandinavian, dreaming in the declining sun? It is twilight; the night comes on, the lamps are lighted in the city below, the stars are kindled in the firmament above, and the tower of Redderholm's church rises aloft towards the starry space. The stars shine through there; it is as if cut in lace, but every thread is of cast-iron and of the thickness of beams.

We go down there, and in there, in the stilly eve.—A world of spirits reigns within. See, in the vaulted isles, on carved wooden horses, sits armour, that was once borne by Magnus Ladelaas, Christian the Second, and Charles the Ninth. A thousand flags that once waved to the peal of music and the clang of arms, to the darted javelin and the cannon's roar, moulder away here: they hang in long rags from the staff, and the staves lie cast aside, where the flag has long since become dust. Almost all the Kings of Sweden slumber in silver and copper coffins within these walls. From the altar aisle we look through the open-grated door, in between piled-up drums and hanging flags: here is preserved a bloody tunic, and in the coffin are the remains of Gustavus Adolphus. Who is that dead opposite neighbour in the chapel, across there in the other side-aisle of the church? There, below a glass lid, lies a dress shot through, and on the floor stands a pair of long, thick boots—they belonged to the

---

1   "The Lion in the desert;" i.e. Napoleon.

hero-King, the wanderer, Charles xii., whose realm is now this narrow coffin.

How sacred it is here under this vaulted roof! The mightiest men of centuries are gathered together here, perishable as these moth-eaten flags—mute and yet so eloquent. And without there is life and activity: the world goes on in its old course; generations change in the old houses; the houses change—yet Stockholm is always the heart of Sweden, Birger's city, whose features are continually renewed, continually beautified.

DIURGAERDEN

Diurgaerden is a large piece of land made into a garden by our Lord himself. Come with us over there. We are still in the city, but before the palace lie the broad hewn stone stairs, leading down to the water, where the Dalkulls—i.e., the Dalecarlian women— stand and ring with metal bells. On board! here are boats enough to choose amongst, all with wheels, which the Dalkulls turn. In coarse white linen, red stockings, with green heels, and singularly thick-soled shoes, with the upper-leather right up the shin-bone, stands the Dalkull; she has ornamented the boat, that now shoots away, with green branches. Houses and streets rise and unfold themselves; churches and gardens start forth; they stand on Soedermalm high above the tops of the ships' masts. The scenery reminds one of the Bhosphorus and Pera; the motley dress of the Dalkulls is quite Oriental—and listen! the wind bears melancholy Skalmeie tones out to us. Two poor Dalecarlians are playing music on the quay; they are the same drawn-out, melancholy tones that are played by the Bulgarian musicians in the streets of Pera. We stept out, and are in the Diurgarden.

What a crowd of equipages pass in rows through the broad avenue! and what a throng of well-dressed pedestrians of all classes! One thinks of the garden of the Villa Borghese, when, at the time of the wine feast, the Roman people and strangers take the air there. We are in the Borghese garden; we are by the Bosphorus, and yet far in the North. The pine-tree rises large and free; the birch droops its branches, as the weeping willow alone has power to do—and what magnificently grand oaks! The pine-trees themselves are mighty trees, beautiful to the painter's eye; splendid green grass plains lie stretched before us, and the fiord rolls its green, deep waters close past, as if it were a river. Large ships with swelling sails, the one high above the other, steamers and boats, come and go in varied numbers.

Come! let us up to Bystroem's villa; it lies on the stony cliff up there, where the large oak-trees stand in their stubborn grandeur: we see from here the whole tripartite city, Soedermalm, Nordmalm and the island with that huge palace. It is delightful, the building here on this rock, and the building stands, and that almost entirely of marble, a "Casa santa d'Italia," as if borne through the air here in the North. The walls within are painted in the Pompeian style, but heavy: there is nothing genial. Round about stand large marble figures by Bystroem, which have not, however, the soul of antiquity. Madonna is encumbered by her heavy marble drapery, the girl with the flower-garland is an ugly young thing, and on seeing Hero with the weeping Cupid, one thinks of a *pose* arranged by a ballet-master.

Let us, however, see what is pretty. The little Cupid-seller is pretty, and the stone is made as flexible as life in the waists of the bathing-women. One of them, as she steps out, feels the water with her feet, and we feel, with her, a sensation that the water is cold. The coolness of the marble-hall realizes this feeling. Let us go out into the sunshine, and up to the neighbouring cliff, which rises above the mansions and houses. Here the wild roses shoot forth from the crevices in the rock; the sunbeams fall prettily between the splendid pines and the graceful birches, upon the high grass before the colossal bronze bust of Bellmann. This place was the favourite one of that Scandinavian improvisatore. Here he lay in the grass, composed and sang his anacreontic songs, and here, in the summer-time, his annual festival is held. We will raise his altar here in the red evening sunlight. It is a flaming bowl, raised high on the jolly tun, and it is wreathed with roses. Morits tries his hunting-horn, that which was Oberon's horn in the inn-parlour, and everything danced, from Ulla to "Mutter paa Toppen:"[m] they stamped with their feet and clapped their hands, and clinked the pewter lid of the ale-tankard; "hej kara Sjael! fukta din aske!" (Hey! dear soul! moisten your clay).

---

m   The landlady of an alehouse.

A Teniers' picture became animated, and still lives in song. Morits blows the horn on Bellmann's place around the flowing bowl, and whole crowds dance in a circle, young and old; the carriages too, horses and waggons, filled bottles and clattering tankards: the Bellmann dithyrambic clangs melodiously; humour and low life, sadness—and amongst others, about

"—hur oegat gret
Ved de Cypresser, som stroeddes." [n]

Painter, seize thy brush and palette and paint the Maenade—but not her who treads the winebag, whilst her hair flutters in the wind, and she sings ecstatic songs. No, but the Maenade that ascends from Bellmann's steaming bowl is the Punch's Anadyomene—she, with the high heels to the red shoes, with rosettes on her gown and with fluttering veil and mantilla—fluttering, far too fluttering! She plucks the rose of poetry from her breast and sets it in the ale-can's spout; clinks with the lid, sings about the clang of the hunting horn, about breeches and old shoes and all manner of stuff. Yet we are sensible that he is a true poet; we see two human eyes shining, that announce to us the human heart's sadness and hope.

---

n   How the eyes wept by the cypresses that were strewn around.

A Story

All the apple-trees in the garden had sprung out. They had made haste to get blossoms before they got green leaves; and all the ducklings were out in the yard—and the cat too! He was, so to speak, permeated by the sunshine; he licked it from his own paws; and if one looked towards the fields, one saw the corn standing so charmingly green! And there was such a twittering and chirping amongst all the small birds, just as if it were a great feast. And that one might indeed say it was, for it was Sunday. The bells rang, and people in their best clothes went to church, and looked so pleased. Yes, there was something so pleasant in everything: it was indeed so fine and warm a day, that one might well say: "Our Lord is certainly unspeakably good towards us poor mortals!"

But the clergyman stood in the pulpit in the church, and spoke so loud and so angrily! He said that mankind was so wicked, and that God would punish them for it, and that when they died, the wicked went down into hell, where they would burn for ever; and he said that their worm would never die, and their fire never be extinguished, nor would they ever get rest and peace!

It was terrible to hear, and he said it so determinedly. He described hell to them as a pestilential hole, where all the filthiness of the world flowed together. There was no air except the hot, sulphurous flames; there was no bottom; they sank and sank into everlasting silence! It was terrible, only to hear about it; but the clergyman said it right honestly out of his heart, and all the people in the church were quite terrified. But all the little birds outside

60

the church sang so pleasantly, and so pleased, and the sun shone so warm:—it was as if every little flower said: "God is so wondrous good to us altogether!" Yes, outside it was not at all as the clergyman preached.

In the evening, when it was bed-time, the clergyman saw his wife sit so still and thoughtful.

"What ails you?" said he to her.

"What ails me?" she replied; "what ails me is, that I cannot collect my thoughts rightly—that I cannot rightly understand what you said; that there were so many wicked, and that they should burn eternally!—eternally, alas, how long! I am but a sinful being; but I could not bear the thought in my heart to allow even the worst sinner to burn for ever. And how then should our Lord permit it? he who is so wondrously good, and who knows how evil comes both from without and within. No, I cannot believe it, though you say it."

It was autumn. The leaves fell from the trees; the grave, severe clergyman sat by the bedside of a dying person; a pious believer closed her eyes—it was the clergyman's own wife.

"If any one find peace in the grave, and grace from God, then it is thou," said the clergyman, and he folded her hands, and read a psalm over the dead body.

And she was borne to the grave: two heavy tears trickled down that stern man's cheeks; and it was still and vacant in the parsonage; the sunshine within was extinguished:—she was gone.

It was night. A cold wind blew over the clergyman's head; he opened his eyes, and it was just as if the moon shone into his room. But the moon did not shine. It was a figure which stood before his bed—he saw the spirit of his deceased wife. She looked on him so singularly afflicted; it seemed as though she would say something.

The man raised himself half erect in bed, and stretched his arms out towards her.

"Not even to thee is granted everlasting peace. Thou dost suffer; thou, the best, the most pious!"

And the dead bent her head in confirmation of his words, and laid her hand on her breast.

"And can I procure you peace in the grave?"

"Yes!" it sounded in his ear.

"And how?"

"Give me a hair, but a single hair of the head of that sinner, whose fire will never be quenched; that sinner whom God will cast down into hell, to everlasting torment."

"Yes; so easily thou canst be liberated, thou pure, thou pious one!" said he.

"Then follow me," said the dead; "it is so granted us. Thou canst be by my side, wheresoever thy thoughts will. Invisible to mankind, we stand in their most secret places; but thou must point with a sure hand to the one destined to eternal punishment, and ere the cock crow he must be found."

And swift, as if borne on the wings of thought, they were in the great city, and the names of the dying sinners shone from the walls of the houses in letters of fire: "Arrogance, Avarice, Drunkenness, Voluptuousness;" in short, sin's whole seven-coloured arch.

"Yes, in there, as I thought it, as I knew it," said the clergyman, "are housed those condemned to eternal fire."

And they stood before the splendidly-illumined portico, where the broad stairs were covered with carpets and flowers, and the music of the dance sounded through the festal saloons. The porter stood there in silk and velvet, with a large silver-headed stick.

"*Our* ball can match with the King's," said he, and turned towards the crowd in the street—his magnificent thoughts were visible in his whole person. "Poor devils! who stare in at the portico, you are altogether ragamuffins, compared to me!"

"Arrogance," said the dead; "dost thou see him?"

"Him!" repeated the clergyman; "he is a simpleton—a fool only, and will not be condemned to eternal fire and torment."

"A fool only," sounded through the whole house of Arrogance.

And they flew into the four bare walls of Avarice, where skinny, meagre, shivering with cold, hungry and thirsty, the old man clung fast with all his thoughts to his gold. They saw how he, as in a fever, sprang from his wretched pallet, and took a loose stone out of the wall. There lay gold coins in a stocking-foot; he fumbled at his ragged tunic, in which gold coins were sewed fast, and his moist fingers trembled.

"He is ill: it is insanity; encircled by fear and evil dreams."

And they flew away in haste, and stood by the criminals' wooden couch, where they slept side by side in long rows. One of them started up from his sleep like a wild animal, and uttered a hideous scream: he struck his companion with his sharp elbow, and the latter turned sleepily round.

"Hold your tongue, you beast, and sleep! this is your way every night! Every night!" he repeated; "yes, you come every night, howling and choking me! I have done one thing or another in a passion; I was born with a passionate temper, and it has brought me in here a second time; but if I have done wrong, so have I also got my punishment. But one thing I have not confessed. When I last went out from here, and passed by my master's farm, one thing and another boiled up in me, and I directly stroked a lucifer against the wall: it came a little too near the thatch, and everything was burnt—hotheadedness came over it, just as it comes over me, I helped to save the cattle and furniture. Nothing living was burnt, except a flock of pigeons: they flew into the flames, and the yard dog. I had not thought of the dog. I could hear it howl, and that howl I always hear yet, when I would sleep; and if I do get to sleep, the dog comes also—so large and hairy! He lies down on me, howls, and strangles me! Do but hear what I am telling you. Snore—yes, that you can—snore the whole night through, and I not even a quarter of an hour!"

And the blood shone from the eyes of the fiery one; he fell on his companion, and struck him in the face with his clenched fist.

"Angry Mads has become mad again!" resounded on all sides, and the other rascals seized hold of him, wrestled with him, and bent him double, so that his head was forced between his legs, where they bound it fast, so that the blood was nearly springing out of his eyes, and all the pores.

"You will kill him!" said the clergyman,—"poor unfortunate!" and as he stretched his hands out over him, who had already suffered too severely, in order to prevent further mischief, the scene changed.

They flew through rich halls, and through poor chambers; voluptuousness and envy, all mortal sins strode past them. A recording angel read their sin and their defence; this was assuredly little for God, for God reads the heart; He knows perfectly the evil that comes within it and from without, He, grace, all-loving kindness. The hand of the clergyman trembled: he did not venture to stretch it out, to pluck a hair from the sinner's head. And the tears streamed down from his eyes, like the waters of *grace* and love, which quenched the eternal fire of hell.

The cock then crowed.

"Merciful God! Thou wilt grant her that peace in the grave which I have not been able to redeem."

"That I now have!" said the dead; "it was thy hard words, thy dark, human belief of God and his creatures, which drove me to thee! Learn to know mankind; even in the bad there is a part of God—a part that will conquer and quench the fire of hell."

And a kiss was pressed on the clergyman's lips:—it shone around him. God's clear, bright sun shone into the chamber, where his wife, living, mild, and affectionate, awoke him from a dream, sent from God!

UPSALA

It is commonly said, that Memory is a young girl with light blue eyes. Most poets say so; but we cannot always agree with most poets. To us memory comes in quite different forms, all according to that land, or that town to which she belongs. Italy sends her as a charming Mignon, with black eyes and a melancholy smile, singing Bellini's soft, touching songs. From Scotland Memory's sprite appears as a powerful lad with bare knees; the plaid hangs over his shoulder, the thistle-flower is fixed on his cap; Burns's songs then fill the air like the heath-lark's song, and Scotland's wild thistle flowers beautifully fragrant as the fresh rose. But now for Memory's sprite from Sweden, from Upsala. He comes thence in the form of a student—at least, he wears the Upsala student's white cap with the black rim. To us it points out its home, as the Phrygian cap denotes Ganymede.

It was in the year 1843, that the Danish students travelled to Upsala. Young hearts met together; eyes sparkled: they laughed, they sang. Young hearts are the future—the conquering future—in the beautiful, true and good; it is so good that brothers should know and love each other. Friendship's meeting is still annually remembered in the palace-yard of Upsala, before the monument of Gustavus Vasa—by the hurra! for Denmark, in warm-hearted compliment to me.

Two summers afterwards, the visit was returned. The Swedish students came to Copenhagen, and that they might there be known amongst the multitude, the Upsala students wore a white cap with a black rim: this cap is accordingly a memorial,—the sign of friendship's bridge over that river of blood which once flowed between kindred nations. When one meets in heart and spirit, a blissful seed is then sown. Memory's sprite, come to us! we know thee by the cap from Upsala: be thou our guide, and from our more southern home, after years and days, we will make the voyage over again, quicker than if we flew in Doctor Faustus' magic cloak. We are in Stockholm: we stand on the Ridderholm where the steamers lie alongside the bulwarks: one of them sends forth clouds of thick smoke from its chimney; the deck is crowded with passengers, and the white cap with the black rim is not wanting.

We are off to Upsala; the paddles strike the waters of the Maelar, and we shoot away from the picturesque city of Stockholm. The whole voyage, direct to Upsala, is a kaleidescope on a large scale. It is true, there is nothing of the magical in the scenery, but landscape gives place to landscape, and clouds and sunshine refresh their variegated beauty. The Maelar lake curves, is compressed, and widens again: it is as if one passed from lake to lake through narrow canals and broad rivers. Sometimes it appears as if the lake ended in small rivulets between dark pines and rocks, when suddenly another large lake, surrounded by corn fields and meadows, opens itself to view: the light-green linden trees, which have just unfolded their leaves, shine forth before the dark grey rocks. Again a new lake opens before us, with islets, trees and red painted houses, and during the whole voyage there is a lively arrival and departure of passengers, in flat bottomed boats, which are nearly upset in the billowy wake of the vessel.

It appears most dangerous opposite to Sigtuna, Sweden's old royal city: the lake is broad here; the waves rise as if they were the waters of the ocean; the boats rock—it is fearful to look at! But here there must be a calm; and Sigtuna, that little interesting town where the old towers stand in ruins, like outposts along the rocks, reflects itself in the water.

We fly past! and now we are in Tyris rivulet! Part of a meadow is flooded; a herd of horses become shy from the snorting of the steamer's engine; they dash through the water in the meadow, and it spurts up all over them. It glitters there between the trees on the declivity: the Upsala students lie encamped there, and exercise themselves in the use of arms.

The rivulet forms a bay, and the high plain extends itself. We see old Upsala's hills; we see Upsala's city with its church, which, like Notre Dame, raises its stony arms towards heaven. The university rises to the view, in appearance half palace and half barracks, and there aloft, on the greensward-clothed bank, stands the old red-painted huge palace with its towers.

We stop at the bulwark near the arched bridge, and so go on shore. Whither wilt thou conduct us first, thou our guide with the white-and-black student's cap? Shall we go up to the palace, or to Linnaeus's garden! or shall we go to the church-yard where the nettles grow over Geier's and Toernro's graves? No, but to the young and the living Upsala's life—the students. Thou tellest us about them; we hear the heart's pulsations, and our hearts beat in sympathy!

In the first year of the war between Denmark and the insurgents, many a brave Upsala student left his quiet, comfortable home, and entered the ranks with his Danish brothers. The Upsala students gave up their most joyous festival—the May-day festival—and the money they at other times used to contribute annually towards the celebration thereof, they sent to the Danes, after the sum had been increased by concerts which were given in Stockholm and Vesteraas. That circumstance will not be forgotten in Denmark.

Upsala student, thou art dear to us by thy disposition! thou art dear to us from thy lively jests! We will mention a trait thereof. In Upsala, it had become the fashion to be Hegelianers—that is to say, always to interweave Hegel's philosophical terms in conversation. In order to put down this practice, a few clever fellows took upon themselves the task of hammering some of the most difficult technical words into the memory of a humorous and commonly drunken country innkeeper, at whose house many a *Sexa* was often held; and the man spoke Hegelianic in his mellow hours, and the effect was so absurd, that the employment of philosophical scraps in his speech was ridiculed, understood, and the nuisance abandoned.

Beautiful songs resound as we approach: we hear Swedish, Norwegian and Danish. The melody's varied beacon makes known to us where Upsala's students are assembled. The song proceeds from the assembly-room—from the tavern saloon, and like serenades in the silent evening, when a young friend departs, or a dear guest is honoured. Glorious melodies! ye enthral, so that we forget that the sun goes down, and the moon rises.

"Herre min Gud hvad din Manen lyser
Se, hvilken Glands ut ofver Land och Stad!"

is now sung, and we see:

"Hoegt opp i Slottet hvarenda ruta
Blixtrar some vore den en aedelsten." [o]

Up thither then is our way! lead us, memory's sprite, into the palace, the courteous governor of Upland's dwelling; mild glances greet us; we see dear beings in a happy circle, and all the leading characters of Upsala. We again see him whose cunning quickened our perceptions as to the mysteries of vegetable life, so that even the toad-stool is unveiled to us as a building more artfully constructed than the labyrinths of the olden time. We see "The Flowers'" singer, he who led us to "The Island of Bliss;" we meet with him whose popular lays are borne on melodies into the world; his wife by his side. That quiet, gentle woman with those faithful eyes is the daughter of Frithiof's bard; we see noble men and women, ladies of the high nobility, with sounding and significant family names with *silver* and *lilies,—stars* and *swords*.

Hark! listen to that lively song. Gunnar Wennerberg, Gluntarra's poet and composer, sings his songs with Boronees,[p] and they acquire a dramatic life and reality.

How spiritual and enjoyable! one becomes happy here, one feels proud of the age one lives in, happy in being distant from the horrible tragedies that history speaks of within these walls.

We can hear about them when the song is silent, when those friendly forms disappear, and the festal lights are extinguished: from the pages of history that tale resounds with a clang of horror. It was in those times, which the many still call poetic—the romantic middle ages—that bards sang of its most brilliant periods, and covered with the radiance of their genius the sanguinary gulf

---

o   Lord, my God, how Thy moon shines! See what lustre over land and city! High up in the palace every pane glistens as if it were a gem.

p   Gluntarra duets, by Gunnar Wennerberg.

of brutality and superstition. Terror seizes us in Upsala's palace: we stand in the vaulted hall, the wax tapers burn from the walls, and King Erik the Fourteenth sits with Saul's dark despondency, with Cain's wild looks. Niels Sture occupies his thoughts, the recollection of injustice exercised against him lashes his conscience with scourges and scorpions, as deadly terrible as they are revealed to us in the page of history.

King Erik the Fourteenth, whose gloomy distrust often amounted to insanity, thought that the nobility aimed at his life. His favourite, Goran Persson, found it to his advantage to strengthen him in this belief. He hated most the popularly favoured race of the Stures, and of them, the light-haired Niels Sture in particular; for Erik thought that he had read in the stars that a man with light hair should hurl him from the throne; and as the Swedish General after the lost battle of Svarteaa, laid the blame on Niels Sture, Erik directly believed it, yet dared not to act as he desired, but even gave Niels Sture royal presents. Yet because he was again accused by one single person of having checked the advance of the Swedish army at Baehues, Erik invited him to his palace at Svartsjoe, gave him an honourable place at his royal table, and let him depart in apparent good faith for Stockholm, where, on his arrival, the heralds were ordered to proclaim in the streets: "Niels Sture is a traitor to his country!"

There Goran Persson and the German retainers seized him, and sat him by force on the executioner's most miserable hack; struck him in the face so that the blood streamed down, placed a tarred straw crown on his head, and fastened a paper with derisive words, on the saddle before him. They then let a row of hired beggar-boys and old fish-wives go in couples before, and to the tail of the horse they bound two fir-trees, the roots of which dragged on the ground and swept the street after the traitor. Niels Sture exclaimed that he had not deserved this treatment from his King and he begged the groom, who went by his side, and had served him in the field of battle, to attest the truth like an honest man; when they all shouted aloud, that he suffered innocently, and had acted like a true Swede. But the procession was driven forward through the streets without stopping, and at night Niels Sture was conducted to prison.

King Erik sits in his royal palace: he orders the torches and candles to be lighted, but they are of no avail—his thoughts' scorpions sting his soul.

"I have again liberated Niels Sture," he mutters; "I have had placards put up at every street-corner, and let the heralds proclaim that no one shall dare to speak otherwise than well of Niels Sture! I have sent him on an honourable mission to a foreign court, in order to sue for me in marriage! He has had reparation enough made to him; but never will he, nor his mighty race, forget the derision and shame I have made him suffer. They will all betray me—kill me!"

And King Erik commands that all Sture's kindred shall be made prisoners.

King Erik sits in his royal palace: the sun shines, but not into the King's heart. Niels Sture enters the chamber with an answer of consent from the royal bride, and the King shakes him by the hand, making fair promises—and the following evening Niels Sture is a prisoner in Upsala Palace.

King Erik's gloomy mind is disturbed; he has no rest; he has no peace, between fear and distrust. He hurries away to Upsala Palace; he will make all straight and just again by marrying Niels Sture's sister. Kneeling, he begs her imprisoned father's consent, and obtains it; but in the very moment, the spirit of distrust is again upon him, and he cries in his insanity:

"But you will not forgive me the shame I brought on Niels!"

At the same time, Goran Persson announced that King Erik's brother, John, had escaped from his prison, and that a revolt was breaking out. And Erik ran, with a sharp dagger into Niels Sture's prison.

"Art thou there, traitor to thy country!" he shouted, and thrust the dagger into Shire's arm; and Sture drew it out again, wiped off the blood, kissed the hilt, and returned the weapon to the King, saying:

"Be lenient with me, Sire; I have not deserved your disfavour."

Erik laughed aloud.

"Ho! ho! do but hear the villain! how he can pray for himself!"

And the King's halberdier stuck his lance through Niels Sture's eye, and thus gave him his death. Sture's blood cleaves to Upsala Palace—to King Erik always and everlastingly. No church masses can absolve his soul from that base crime.

Let us now go to the church.

A little flight of stairs in the side aisle leads us up to a vaulted chamber, where kings' crowns and sceptres, taken from the coffins of the dead, are deposited in wooden closets. Here, in the corner, hangs Niels Sture's blood-covered clothes and knight's hat, on the outside of which a small silk glove is fastened. It was his betrothed one's dainty glove—that which he, knight-like, always bore.

O, barbarous era! highly vaunted as you are in song, retreat, like the storm-cloud, and be poetically beautiful to all who do not see thee in thy true light.

We descend from the little chamber, from the gold and silver of the dead, and wander in the church's aisles. The cold marble tombs, with shields of arms and names, awaken other, milder thoughts.

The walls shine brightly, and with varied hues, in the great chapel behind the high altar. The fresco paintings present to us the most eventful circumstances of Gustavus Vasa's life. Here his clay moulders, with that of his three consorts. Yonder, a work in marble, by Sargel, solicits our attention: it adorns the burial-chapel of the De Geers; and here, in the centre aisle, under that flat stone, rests Linnaeus. In the side chapel, is his monument, erected by *amici* and *discipuli:* a sufficient sum was quickly raised for its erection, and the King, Gustavus the Third, himself brought his royal gift. The projector of the subscription then explained to him, that the purposed inscription was, that the monument was erected only by friends and disciples, and King Gustavus answered: "And am not I also one of Linnaeus's disciples?"

The monument was raised, and a hall built in the botanical garden, under splendid trees. There stands his bust; but the remembrance of himself, his home, his own little garden—where is it most vivid? Lead us thither.

On yonder side of Fyri's rivulet, where the street forms a declivity, where red-painted, wooden houses boast their living grass roofs, as fresh as if they were planted terraces, lies Linnaeus's garden. We stand within it. How solitary! how overgrown! Tall nettles shoot up between the old, untrimmed, rank hedges. No water-plants appear more in that little, dried-up basin; the hedges that were formerly clipped, put forth fresh leaves without being checked by the gardener's shears.

It was between these hedges that Linnaeus at times saw his own double—that optical illusion which presents the express image of a second self—from the hat to the boots.

Where a great man has lived and worked, the place itself becomes, as it were, a part and parcel of him: the whole, as well as a part, has mirrored itself in his eye; it has entered into his soul, and become linked with it and the whole world.

We enter the orangeries: they are now transformed into assembly-rooms; the blooming winter-garden has disappeared; but the walls yet show a sort of herbarium. They are hung round with the portraits of learned Swedes—herbarium from the garden of science and knowledge. Unknown faces—and, to the stranger, the greatest part are unknown names—meet us here.

One portrait amongst the many attracts our attention: it looks singular; it is the half-length figure of an old man in a shirt, lying in his bed. It is that of the learned theologian, Oedmann, who after he had been compelled to keep his bed by a fever, found himself so comfortable in it, that he continued to lie there during the remainder of his long life, and was not to be induced to get up. Even when the next house was burning, they were obliged to carry him out in his bed into the street. Death and cold were his two bugbears. The cold would kill him, was his opinion; and so, when the students came with their essays and treatises, the manuscripts were warmed at the stove before he read them. The windows of his room were never opened, so that there was a suffocating and impure air in his dwelling. He had a writing-desk on the bed; books and manuscripts lay in confusion round about; dishes, plates, and pots stood here or there, as the convenience of the moment dictated, and his only companion was a deaf and dumb laughter.

She sat still in a corner by the window, wrapped up in herself, and staring before her, as if she were a figure that had flown out of the frame around the dark, mouldy canvas, which had once shown a picture on the wall.

Here, in the room, in this impure atmosphere, the old man lived happily, and reached his seventieth year, occupied with the translation of travels in Africa. This tainted atmosphere, in which he lay, became, to his conceit, the dromedary's high back, which lifted him aloft in the burning sun; the long, hanging-down cobwebs were the palm-trees' waving banners, and the caravan went over rivers to the wild bushmen. Old Oedmann was with the hunters, chasing the elephants in the midst of the thick reeds; the agile tiger-cat sprang past, and the serpents shone like garlands around the boughs of the trees: there was excitement, there was danger—and yet he lay so comfortably in his good and beloved bed in Upsala.

One winter's day, it happened that a Dalecarlian peasant mistook the house, and came into Oedmann's chamber in his snow-covered skin cloak, and with his beard full of ice. Oedmann shouted to him to go his way, but the peasant was deaf, and therefore stepped quite close up to the bed. He was the personification of Winter himself, and Oedmann fell ill from this visit: it was his only sickness during the many years he lay here as a polypus, grown fast, and where he was painted, as we see his portrait in the assembly-room.

From the hall of learning we will go to its burial-place—that is to say, its open burial-place—the great library. We wander from hall to hall, up stairs and down stairs. Along the shelves, behind them and round about, stand books, those petrifactions of the mind, which might again be vivified by spirit. Here lives a kind-hearted and mild old man, the librarian, Professor Schroeder. He smiles and nods as he hears how memory's sprite takes his place here as guide, and tells of and shows, as we see, Tegner's copy and translation of Ochlenschloeger's "Hakon Jarl and Palnatoke." We see Vadstene cloister's library, in thick hog's leather bindings, and think of the fair hands of the nuns that have borne them, the pious, mild eyes that conjured the spirit out of the dead letters. Here is the celebrated Codex Argentius, the translation of the "Four Evangelists."[q] Gold and silver letters glisten from the red parchment leaves. We see ancient Icelandic manuscripts, from de la Gardie's refined French saloon, and Thauberg's Japanese manuscripts. By merely looking at these books, their bindings and names, one at last becomes, as it were, quite worm-eaten in spirit, and longs to be out in the free air—and we are there; by Upsala's ancient hills. Thither do thou lead us, remembrance's elf, out of the city, out on the far extended plain, where Denmark's church stands—the church that was erected from

---

q   A Gothic translation of the Four Evangelists, and ascribed to the Moesogothic Archbishop Ulphilas.

the booty which the Swedes gained in the war against the Danes. We follow the broad high road: it leads us close past Upsala's old hills—Odin's, Thor's and Freia's graves, as they are called.

There once stood ancient Upsala, here now are but a few peasants' farms. The low church, built of granite blocks, dates from a very remote age; it stands on the remains of the heathen temple. Each of the hills is a little mountain, yet each was raised by human hands. Letters an ell long, and whole names, are cut deep in the thin greensward, which the new sprouting grass gradually fills up. The old housewife, from the peasant's cot close by the hill, brings the silver-bound horn, a gift of Charles John xiv., filled with mead. The wanderer empties the horn to the memory of the olden time, for Sweden, and for the heart's constant thoughts— young love!

Yes, thy toast is drunk here, and many a beauteous rose has been remembered here with a heartfelt hurra! and years after, when the same wanderer again stood here, she, the blooming rose, had been laid in the earth; the spring roses had strown their leaves over her coffined clay; the sweet music of her lips sounded but in memory; the smile in her eyes and around her mouth, was gone like the sunbeams, which then shone on Upsala's hills. Her name in the greensward is grown over; she herself is in the earth, and it is closed above her; but the hill here, closed for a thousand years, is open.

Through the passage which is dug deep into the hills, we come to the funereal urns which contain the bones of youthful kindred; the dust of kings, the gods of the earth.

The old housewife, from the peasant's cot, has lighted half a hundred wax candles and placed them in rows in the otherwise pitchy-dark, stone-paved passage. It shines so festally in here over the bones of the olden time's mighty ones, bones that are now charred and burnt to ashes. And whose were they? Thou world's power and glory, thou world's posthumous fame—dust, dust like beauty's rose, laid in the dark earth, where no light shines; thy memorials are but a name, the name but a sound. Away hence, and up on the hill where the wind blows, the sun shines, and the eye looks over the green plain, to the sunlit, dear Upsala, the student's city.

SALA

Sweden's great King, Germany's preserver, Gustavus Adolphus, founded Sala. The little wood, close by, still preserves legends of the heroic King's youthful love—of his meeting here with Ebba Brahe.

Sala's silver mines are the largest, the deepest, and oldest in Sweden: they reach to the depth of one hundred and seventy fathoms, consequently they are almost as deep as the Baltic. This of itself is enough to awaken an interest for a little town; but what is its appearance? "Sala," says the guide-book, "lies in a valley, in a flat, and not very pleasant district." And so truly it is: it was not very attractive approaching it our way, and the high road led directly into the town, which is without any distinctive character. It consists of a long street with what we may term a nucleus and a few fibres. The nucleus is the market-place, and the fibres are the few lanes diverging from it. The long street—that is to say, long in a little town—is quite without passengers; no one comes out from the doors, no one is to be seen at the windows.

It was therefore with pleased surprise that I at length descried a human being: it was at an ironmonger's, where there hung a paper of pins, a handkerchief and two tea-pots in the window. There I saw a solitary shop-boy, standing quite still, but leaning over the counter and looking out of the open door. He certainly wrote in his journal, if he had one, in the evening: "To-day a traveller drove through the town; who he was, God knows, for I don't!"—yes, that was what the shop-boy's face said, and an honest face it was.

In the inn at which I arrived, there was the same grave-like stillness as in the street. The gate was certainly closed, but all the inner doors were wide open; the farm-yard cock stood uplifted in the middle of the traveller's room and crowed, in order to show that there was somebody at home. The house, however, was quite picturesque: it had an open balcony, from which one might look out upon the yard, for it would have been far too lively had it been facing the street. There hung the old sign and creaked in the wind, as if to show that it at least was alive. I saw it from my window; I saw also how the grass in the street had got the mastery over the pavement. The sun shone brightly, but shone as into the bachelor's solitary room, and on the old maid's balsams in the flower-pots. It was as still as a Scotch Sunday—and yet it was a Tuesday. One was disposed for Young's "Night Thoughts."

I looked out from the balcony into the neighbouring yard: there was not a soul to be seen, but children had been playing there. There was a little garden made of dry sticks: they were stuck down in the soft soil and had been watered; a broken pan, which had certainly served by way of watering-pot, lay there still. The sticks signified roses and geraniums.

It had been a delightful garden—alas, yes! We great, grown-up men—we play just so: we make ourselves a garden with what we call love's roses and friendship's geraniums; we water them with our tears and with our heart's blood; and yet they are, and remain, dry sticks without root. It was a gloomy thought; I felt it, and in order to get the dry sticks in my thoughts to blossom, I went out. I wandered in the fibres and in the long threads—that is to say, in the small lanes—and in the great street; and here was more life than I dared to expect. I met a herd of cattle returning or going—which I know not—for they were without a herdsman. The shop-boy still stood behind the counter, leaned over it and greeted me; the stranger took his hat off again—that was my day's employment in Sala.

Pardon me, thou silent town, which Gustavus Adolphus built, where his young heart felt the first emotions of love, and where the silver lies in the deep shafts—that is to say, outside the town, "in a flat, and not very pleasant district."

I knew no one in the town; I had no one to be my guide, so I accompanied the cows, and came to the churchyard. The cows went past, but I stepped over the stile, and stood amongst the graves, where the grass grew high, and almost all the tombstones lay with worn-out inscriptions. On a few only the date of the year was legible. "Anno"—yes, what then? And who rested here? Everything on the stone was erased—blotted out like the earthly life of those mortals that here were earth in earth. What life's dream have ye dead played here in silent Sala?

The setting sun shone over the graves; not a leaf moved on the trees; all was still—still as death—in the city of the silver-mines, of which this traveller's reminiscence is but a frame around the shop-boy who leaned over the counter.

The Mute Book

B y the high road into the forest there stood a solitary farm-house.
Our way lay right through the farm-yard; the sun shone; all
the windows were open; there was life and bustle within, but in the
yard, in an arbour of flowering lilacs, there stood an open coffin. The
corpse had been placed out here, and it was to be buried that fore-
noon. No one stood by and wept over that dead man; no one hung
sorrowfully over him; his face was covered with a white cloth, and
under his head there lay a large, thick book, every leaf of which was
a whole sheet of grey paper, and between each lay withered flowers,
deposited and forgotten—a whole herbarium, gathered in different
places. He himself had requested that it should be laid in the grave
with him. A chapter of his life was blended with every flower.

"Who is that dead man?" we asked, and the answer was: "The old
student from Upsala. They say he was once very clever; he knew the
learned languages, could sing and write verses too; but then there
was something that went wrong, and so he gave both his thoughts
and himself up to drinking spirits, and as his health suffered by it,
he came out here into the country, where they paid for his board and
lodging.

"He was as gentle as a child, when the dark humour did not
come over him, for then he was strong, and ran about in the forest
like a hunted deer; but when we got him home, we persuaded him to
look into the book with the dry plants. Then he would sit the whole
day and look at one plant, and then at another, and many a time the
tears ran down his cheeks. God knows what he then thought! But

he begged that he might have the book with him in his coffin; and now it lies there, and the lid will soon be fastened down, and then he will take his peaceful rest in the grave!"

They raised the winding-sheet. There was peace in the face of the dead: a sunbeam fell on it; a swallow in its arrowy flight, darted into the new-made arbour, and in its flight circled twittering over the dead man's head.

How strange it is!—we all assuredly know it—to take out old letters from the days of our youth and read them: a whole life, as it were, then rises up with all its hopes, and all its troubles. How many of those with whom we, in their time, lived so devotedly, are now even as the dead to us, and yet they still live! But we have not thought of them for many years—them whom we once thought we should always cling to, and share our mutual joys and sorrows with.

The withered oak-leaf in the book here, is a memorial of the friend—the friend of his school-days—the friend for life. He fixed this leaf on the student's cap in the green wood, when the vow of friendship was concluded for the whole of life. Where does he now live? The leaf is preserved; friendship forgotten. Here is a foreign conservatory-plant, too fine for the gardens of the North—it looks as if there still were fragrance in these leaves!—*she* gave it to him—she, the young lady of that noble garden.

Here is the marsh-lotus which he himself has plucked and watered with salt tears—the marsh-lotus from the fresh waters. And here is a nettle: what does its leaf say? What did he think on plucking it—on preserving it? Here are lilies of the valley from the woodland solitudes; here are honeysuckle leaves from the village ale-house flower-pot; and here the bare, sharp blade of grass.

The flowering lilac bends its fresh, fragrant clusters over the dead man's head; the swallow again flies past; "quivit! quivit!" Now the men come with nails and hammer; the lid is placed over the corpse, whose head rests on the Mute-Book—preserved—forgotten!

THE ZÆTHER DALE

Everything was in order, the carriage examined, even a whip
with a good lash was not forgotten. "Two whips would be best,"
said the ironmonger, who sold it, and the ironmonger was a man
of experience, which travellers often are not. A whole bag full of
"slanter"—that is, copper coins of small value—stood before us for
bridge-money, for beggars, for shepherd's boys, or whoever might
open the many field-gates for us that obstructed our progress. But
we had to do this ourselves, for the rain pattered down and lashed
the ground; no one had any desire to come out in such weather.
The rushes in the marsh bent and waved; it was a real rain feast
for them, and it whistled from the tops of the rushes: "We drink
with our feet, we drink with our heads, we drink with the whole
body, and yet we stand on one leg, hurra! We drink with the bending willow, with the dripping flowers on the bank; their cups run
over—the marsh marigold, that fine lady, can bear it better! Hurra!
it is a feast! it pours, it pours; we whistle and we sing; it is our own
song. Tomorrow the frogs will croak the same after us and say, 'it
is quite new!'"

And the rushes waved, and the rain pattered down with a splash-
ing noise—it was fine weather to travel in to Zaether Dale, and to
see its far-famed beauties. The whip-lash now came off the whip; it
was fastened on again, and again, and every time it was shorter, so
that at last there was not a lash, nor was there any handle, for the
handle went after the lash—or sailed after it—as the road was quite
navigable, and gave one a vivid idea of the beginning of the deluge.

One poor jade now drew too much, the other drew too little, and one of the splinter bars broke; well, by all that is vexatious, that was a fine drive! The leather apron in front had a deep pond in its folds with an outlet into one's lap. Now one of the linch-pins came out; now the twisting of the rope harness became loose, and the cross-strap was tired of holding any longer. Glorious inn in Zaether, how I now long more for thee than thy far-famed dale. And the horses went slower, and the rain fell faster, and so—yes, so we were not yet in Zaether.

Patience, thou lank spider, that in the ante-chamber quietly dost spin thy web over the expectant's foot, spin my eyelids close in a sleep as still as the horse's pace! Patience? no, she was not with us in the carriage to Zaether. But to the inn, by the road side, close to the far-famed valley, I got at length, towards evening.

And everything was flowing in the yard, chaotically mingled; manure and farming implements, staves and straw. The poultry sat there washed to shadows, or at least like stuck-up hens' skins with feathers on, and even the ducks crept close up to the wet wall, sated with the wet. The stable-man was cross, the girl still more so; it was difficult to get them to bestir themselves: the steps were crooked, the floor sloping and but just washed, sand strewn thickly on it, and the air was damp and cold. But without, scarcely twenty paces from the inn, on the other side of the road, lay the celebrated valley, a garden made by nature herself, and whose charm consists of trees and bushes, wells and purling brooks.

It was a long hollow; I saw the tops of the trees looming up, and the rain drew its thick veil over it. The whole of that long evening did I sit and look upon it during that shower of showers. It was as if the Venern, the Vettern and a few more lakes ran through an immense sieve from the clouds. I had ordered something to eat and drink, but I got nothing. They ran up and they ran down; there was a hissing sound of roasting by the hearth; the girls chattered, the men drank "sup," [r] strangers came, were shown into their rooms, and got both roast and boiled. Several hours had passed, when I made a forcible appeal to the girl, and she answered phlegmatically: "Why, Sir, you sit there and write without stopping, so you cannot have time to eat."

It was a long evening, "but the evening passed!" It had become quite still in the inn; all the travellers, except myself, had again

---

r   Swedish, sup. Danish, snaps. German, schnaps. English, drams.

departed, certainly in order to find better quarters for the night at Hedemore or Brunbeck. I had seen, through the half-open door into the dirty tap-room, a couple of fellows playing with greasy cards; a huge dog lay under the table and glared with its large red eyes; the kitchen was deserted; the rooms too; the floor was wet, the storm rattled, the rain beat against the windows—"and now to bed! said I."

I slept an hour, perhaps two, and was awakened by a loud bawling from the high road. I started up: it was twilight, the night at that period is not darker—it was about one o'clock. I heard the door shaken roughly; a deep manly voice shouted aloud, and there was a hammering with a cudgel against the planks of the yard-gate. Was it an intoxicated or a mad man that was to be let in? The gate was now opened, but many words were not exchanged. I heard a woman scream at the top of her voice from terror. There was now a great bustling about; they ran across the yard in wooden shoes; the bellowing of cattle and the rough voices of men were mingled together. I sat on the edge of the bed. Out or in! what was to be done? I looked from the window; in the road there was nothing to be seen, and it still rained. All at once some one came up stairs with heavy footsteps: he opened the door of the room adjoining mine—now he stood still! I listened—a large iron bolt fastened my door. The stranger now walked across the floor, now he shook my door, and then kicked against it with a heavy foot, and whilst all this was passing, the rain beat against the windows, and the blast made them rattle.

"Are there any travellers here?" shouted a voice; "the house is on fire!"

I now dressed myself and hastened out of the room and down the stairs. There was no smoke to be seen, but when I reached the yard, I saw that the whole building—a long and extensive one of wood—was enveloped in flames and clouds of smoke. The fire had originated in the baking oven, which no one had looked to; a travel-ler, who accidently came past, saw it, called out and hammered at the door: and the women screamed, and the cattle bellowed, when the fire stuck its red tongue into them.

Now came the fire-engine and the flames were extinguished. By this time it was morning. I stood in the road, scarcely a hundred steps from the far-famed dale. "One may as well spring into it as walk into it!" and I sprang into it; and the rain poured down, and the water flowed—the whole dale was a well.

The trees turned their leaves the wrong side out, purely because of the pouring rain, and they said, as the rushes did the day before: "We drink with our heads, we drink with our feet, and we drink with the whole body, and yet stand on our legs, hurra! it rains, and it pours; we whistle and we sing; it is our own song—and it is quite new!"

Yes, that the rushes also sang yesterday—but it was the same, ever the same. I looked and looked, and all I know of the beauty of Zaether Dale is, that she had washed herself!

THE MIDSUMMER FESTIVAL IN LACKSAND

Lacksand lay on the other side of the dal-elv which the road now led us over for the third or fourth time. The picturesque bell-tower of red painted beams, erected at a distance from the church, rose above the tall trees on the clayey declivity: old willows hung gracefully over the rapid stream. The floating bridge rocked under us—nay, it even sank a little, so that the water splashed under the horse's hoofs; but these bridges have such qualities! The iron chains that held it rattled, the planks creaked, the boards splashed, the water rose, and murmured and roared, and so we got over where the road slants upwards towards the town. Close opposite here the last year's May-pole still stood with withered flowers. How many hands that bound these flowers are now withered in the grave?

It is far prettier to go up on the sloping bank along the elv, than to follow the straight high-road into the town. The path conducts us, between pasture fields and leaf trees, up to the parsonage, where we passed the evening with the friendly family. The clergyman himself was but lately dead, and his relatives were all in mourning. There was something about the young daughter—I knew not myself what it was—but I was led to think of the delicate flax flower, too delicate for the short northern summer.

They spoke about the Midsummer festival the next day, and of the winter season here, when the swans, often more than thirty at a time, sit (motionless themselves) on the elv, and utter strange, mournful tones. They always come in pairs, they said, two and two, and thus they also fly away again. If one of them dies, its partner always remains a long time after all the others are gone; lingers, laments, and then flies away alone and solitary.

When I left the parsonage in the evening, the moon, in its first quarter, was up. The May-pole was raised; the little steamer, 'Prince Augustus,' with several small vessels in tow, came over the Siljan lake and into the elv; a musician sprang on shore, and began to play dances under the tall wreathed May-pole. And there was soon a merry circle around it—all so happy, as if the whole of life were but a delightful summer night.

Next morning was the Midsummer Festival. It was Sunday, the 24th of June, and a beautiful sunshiny day it was. The most picturesque sight at the festival is to see the people from the different parishes coming in crowds, in large boats over Siljan's lake, and landing on its shores. We drove out to the landing-place, Barkedale, and before we got out of the town, we met whole troops coming from there, as well as from the mountains.

Close by the town of Lacksand, there is a row of low wooden shops on both sides of the way, which only get their interior light through the doorway. They form a whole street, and serve as stables for the parishioners, but also—and it was particularly the case that morning—to go into and arrange their finery. Almost all the shops or sheds were filled with peasant women, who were anxiously busy about their dresses, careful to get them into the right folds, and in the mean time peeped continually out of the door to see who came past. The number of arriving church-goers increased; men, women, and children, old and young, even infants; for at the Midsummer festival no one stays at home to take care of them, and so of course they must come too—all must go to church.

What a dazzling army of colours! Fiery red and grass green aprons meet our gaze. The dress of the women is a black skirt, red bodice, and white sleeves: all of them had a psalm-book wrapped in the folded silk pocket-handkerchief. The little girls were entirely in yellow, and with red aprons; the very least were in Turkish-yellow clothes. The men were dressed in black coats, like our paletots, embroidered with red woollen cord; a red band with a tassel hung down from the large black hat; with dark knee breeches, and blue stockings, with red leather gaiters—in short, there was a dazzling richness of colour, and that, too, on a bright sunny morning in the forest road.

This road led down a steep to the lake, which was smooth and blue. Twelve or fourteen long boats, in form like gondolas, were already drawn up on the flat strand, which here is covered with large stones. These stones served the persons who landed, as bridges; the boats were laid alongside them, and the people clambered up, and went and bore each other on land. There certainly were at least a thousand persons on the strand; and far out on the lake, one could see ten or twelve boats more coming, some with sixteen oars, others with twenty, nay, even with four-and-twenty, rowed by men and women, and every boat decked out with green branches. These, and the varied clothes, gave to the whole an appearance of something so festal, so fantastically rich, as one would hardly think the north possessed. The boats came nearer, all crammed full of living freight; but they came silently, without noise or talking, and rowed up to the declivity of the forest.

The boats were drawn up on the sand: it was a fine subject for a painter, particularly one point—the way up the slope, where the whole mass moved on between the trees and bushes. The most prominent figures there, were two ragged urchins, clothed entirely in bright yellow, each with a skin bundle on his shoulders. They were from Gagne, the poorest parish in Dalecarlia. There was also a lame man with his blind wife: I thought of the fable of my childhood, of the lame and the blind man: the lame man lent his eyes, and the blind his legs, and so they reached the town.

And we also reached the town and the church, and thither they all thronged: they said there were above five thousand persons assembled there. The church-service began at five o'clock. The pulpit and organ were ornamented with flowering lilacs; children sat with lilac-flowers and branches of birch; the little ones had each a piece of oat-cake, which they enjoyed. There was the sacrament for the young persons who had been confirmed; there was organ-playing and psalm-singing; but there was a terrible screaming of children, and the sound of heavy footsteps; the clumsy, iron-shod Dal shoes tramped loudly upon the stone floor. All the church pews, the gallery pews, and the centre aisle were quite filled with people. In the side aisle one saw various groups— playing children, and pious old folks: by the sacristy there sat a young mother giving suck to her child—she was a living image of the Madonna herself.

The first impression of the whole was striking, but only the first—there was too much that disturbed. The screaming of children, and the noise of persons walking were heard above the singing, and besides that, there was an insupportable smell of garlic: almost all the congregation had small bunches of garlic with them, of which they ate as they sat. I could not bear it, and went out into the churchyard: here—as it always is in nature—it was affecting, it was holy. The church door stood open; the tones of the organ, and the voices of the psalm-singers were wafted out here in the bright sunlight, by the open lake: the many who could not find a place in the church, stood outside, and sang with the congregation from the psalm-book: round about on the monuments, which are almost all of cast-iron, there sat mothers suckling their infants—the fountain of life flowed over death and the grave. A young peasant stood and read the inscription on a grave:

> *"Ach hur soedt al hafve lefvet,*
> *Ach hur skjoeut al kunne doee!"* [s]

Beautiful Christian, scriptural language, verses certainly taken from the psalm-book, were read on the graves; they were all read, for the service lasted several hours. This, however, can never be good for devotion.

The crowd at length streamed from the church; the fiery-red and grass-green aprons glittered; but the mass of human beings became thicker, and closer, and pressed forward. The white head-dresses, the white band over the forehead, and the white sleeves, were the prevailing colours—it looked like a long procession in Catholic countries. There was again life and motion on the road; the over-filled boats again rowed away; one waggon drove off after the other; but yet there were people left behind. Married and unmarried men stood in groups in the broad street of Lacksand, from the church up to the inn. I was staying there, and I must acknowledge that my Danish tongue sounded quite foreign to them all. I then tried the Swedish, and the girl at the inn assured me that she understood me better than she had understood the Frenchman, who the year before had spoken French to her.

As I sit in my room, my hostess's grand-daughter, a nice little child, comes in, and is pleased to see my parti-coloured carpet-bag, my Scotch plaid, and the red leather lining of the portmanteau. I di-

s   "How sweet to live—how beautiful to die!"

87

rectly cut out for her, from a sheet of white paper, a Turkish mosque, with minarets and open windows, and away she runs with it—so happy, so happy!

Shortly after, I heard much loud talking in the yard, and I had a presentiment that it was concerning what I had cut out; I therefore stepped softly out into the balcony, and saw the grandmother standing below, and with beaming face, holding my clipped-out paper at arm's length. A whole crowd of Dalecarlians, men and women, stood around, all in artistic ecstacy over my work; but the little girl—the sweet little child—screamed, and stretched out her hands after her lawful property, which she was not permitted to keep, as it was too fine.

I sneaked in again, yet, of course, highly flattered and cheered; but a moment after there was a knocking at my door: it was the grandmother, my hostess, who came with a whole plate full of spice-nuts.

"I bake the best in all Dalecarlia," said she; "but they are of the old fashion, from my grandmother's time. You cut out so well, Sir, should you not be able to cut me out some new fashions?"

And I sat the whole of Midsummer night, and clipped fashions for spice-nuts. Nutcrackers with knights' boots, windmills which were both mill and miller—but in slippers, and with the door in the stomach—and ballet-dancers that pointed with one leg towards the seven stars. Grandmother got them, but she turned the ballet-dancers up and down; the legs went too high for her; she thought that they had one leg and three arms.

"They will be new fashions," said she; "but they are difficult."

FAITH AND KNOWLEDGE

Truth can never be at variance with truth, science can never militate against faith: we naturally speak of them both in their purity: they respond to and they strengthen man's most glorious thought: *immortality*. And yet you may say, "I was more peaceful, I was safer when, as a child, I closed my eyes on my mother's breast and slept without thought or care, wrapping myself up simply in faith." This prescience, this compound of understanding in everything, this entering of the one link into the other from eternity to eternity, tears away from me a support—my confidence in prayer; that which is, as it were, the wings wherewith to fly to my God! If it be loosened, then I fall powerless in the dust, without consolation or hope.

I bend my energies, it is true, towards attaining the great and glorious light of knowledge, but it appears to me that therein is human arrogance: it is, as one should say, "I will be as wise as God." "That you shall be!" said the serpent to our first parents when it would seduce them to eat of the tree of knowledge. Through my understanding I must acknowledge the truth of what the astronomer teaches and proves. I see the wonderful, eternal omniscience of God in the whole creation of the world—in the great and in the small, where the one attaches itself to the other, is joined with the other, in an endless harmonious entireness; and I tremble in my greatest need and sorrow. What can my prayer change, where everything is law, from eternity to eternity?

You tremble as you see the Almighty, who reveals Himself in all loving-kindness—that Creator, according to man's expression, whose understanding and heart are one—you tremble when you know that he has elected you to immortality.

I know it in the faith, in the holy, eternal words of the Bible. Knowledge lays itself like a stone over my grave, but my faith is that which breaks it.

Now, thus it is! The smallest flower preaches from its green stalk, in the name of knowledge—*immortality*. Hear it! the beautiful also bears proofs of immortality, and with the conviction of faith and knowledge, the immortal will not tremble in his greatest need; the wings of prayer will not droop: you will believe in the eternal laws of love, as you believe in the laws of sense.

When the child gathers flowers in the fields and brings us the whole handful, where one is erect and the other hangs the head, thrown as it were among one another, then it is that we see the beauty in every one by itself—that harmony in colour and in form, which pleases our eye so well. We arrange them instinctively, and every single beauty is blended together in one entire beauteous group. We do not look at the flower, but on the whole bouquet. The beauty of harmony is an instinct in us; it lies in our eyes and in our ears, those bridges between our soul and the creation around us—in all our senses there is such a divine, such an entire and perfect stream in our whole being, a striving after the harmonious, as it shows itself in all created things, even in the pulsations of the air, made visible in Chladni's figures.

In the Bible we find the expression: "God in spirit and in truth,"—and hence we most significantly find an expression for the admission of what we call a feeling of the beautiful; for what else is this revelation of God but spirit and truth? And just as our own soul shines out of the eye and the fine movement around the mouth, so does the created image shine forth from God in spirit and truth. There is harmonious beauty from the smallest leaf and flower to the large, swelling bouquet, from our earth itself to the numberless globes in the firmamental space—as far as the eye sees, as far as science ventures, all, small and great, is beauty and harmony.

But if we turn to mankind, for whom we have the highest, the holiest expression; "created in God's image," man, who is able to comprehend and admit in himself all God's creation, the harmony in the harmony then seems to be defective, for at our birth we are all equal! as creatures we have equally "no right to demand;" yet how differently God has granted us abilities! some few so immensely great, others so mean! At our birth God places us in our homes and positions; and to how many of us are allotted the hardest struggles! We are placed *there*, introduced *there*—how many may not say justly: "It were better for me that I had never been born!"

Human life, consequently—the highest here on the earth—does not come under the laws of harmonious beauty: it is inconceivable, it is an injustice, and thus cannot take place.

The defect of harmony in life lies in this:—that we only see a small part thereof, namely, existence here on the earth: there must be a life to come—an immortality.

That, the smallest flower preaches to us, as does all that is created in beauty and harmony.

If our existence ceased with death here, then the most perfect work of God was not perfect; God was not justice and love, as everything in nature and revelation affirms; and if we be referred to the whole of mankind, as that wherein harmony will reveal itself, then our whole actions and endeavours are but as the labours of the coral-insect: mankind becomes but a monument of greatness to the Creator: he would then only have raised His *glory*, not shown His greatest *love*. Loving-kindness is not self-love.

We are immortal! In this rich consciousness we are raised towards God, fundamentally sure, that whatever happens to us, is for our good. Our earthly eye is only able to reach to a certain boundary in space; our soul's eye also has but a limited scope; but beyond *that*, the same laws of loving-kindness must reign, as here. The prescience of eternal omniscience cannot alarm us; we human beings can apprehend the notion thereof in ourselves. We know perfectly what development must take place in the different seasons of the year; the time for flowers and for fruits; what kinds will come forth and thrive; the time of maturity, when the storms must prevail, and when it is the rainy season. Thus must God, in an infinitely greater degree, have the same knowledge of the whole created globes of His universe, as of our earth and the human race here. He must know when that development, that flowering in the human race ordained by Himself, shall come to pass; when the powers of intellect, of full development, are to reign; and under these characters, come to a maturity of development, men will become mighty, driving wheels—every one be the eternal God's likeness indeed.

History shows us these things: joint enters into joint, in the world of spirits, as well as in the materially created world; the eye of wisdom—the all-seeing eye—encompasses the whole! And should we then not be able, in our heart's distress, to pray to this Father with confidence—to pray as the Saviour prayed: "If it be possible, let this cup pass from me; nevertheless, not as I will, but as Thou wilt."

These last words we do not forget! and our prayer will be granted, if it be for our good; or if it be not, then let us, as the child here, that in its trouble comes to its earthly Father, and does not get its wish fulfilled, but is refreshed by mild words, and the affectionate language of reason, so that the eye weeps, which thereby mitigates sorrow, and the child's pain is soothed. This, will prayer also grant us: the eye will be filled with tears, but the heart will be full of consolation! And who has penetrated so deeply into the ways of the soul, that he dare deny that prayer is the wings that bear thee to that sphere of inspiration whence God will extend to thee the olive-branch of help and grace?

By walking with open eyes in the path of knowledge, we see the glory of the Annunciation. The wisdom of generations is but a span on the high pillar of revelation, above which sits the Almighty; but this short span will grow through eternity, in faith and with faith. Knowledge is like a chemical test that pronounces the gold pure!

In the Forest

We are a long way over the elv. We have left the corn-fields behind, and have just come into the forest, where we halt at that small inn, which is ornamented over the doors and windows with green branches for the Midsummer festival. The whole kitchen is hung round with branches of birch and the berries of the mountain-ash: the oat-cakes hang on long poles under the ceiling; the berries are suspended above the head of the old woman who is just scouring her brass kettle bright.

The tap-room, where the peasant sits and carouse, is just as finely hung round with green. Midsummer raises its leafy arbour everywhere, yet it is most flush in the forest—it extends for miles around. Our road goes for miles through that forest, without seeing a house, or the possibility of meeting travellers, driving, riding or walking. Come! The ostler puts fresh horses to the carriage; come with us into the large woody desert: we have a regular trodden way to travel, the air is clear, here is summer's warmth and the fragrance of birch and lime. It is an up and down hill road, always bending, and so, ever changing, but yet always forest scenery—the close, thick forest. We pass small lakes, which lie so still and deep, as if they concealed night and sleep under their dark, glassy surfaces.

We are now on a forest plain, where only charred stumps of trees are to be seen: this long tract is black, burnt, and deserted—not a bird flies over it. Tall, hanging birches now greet us again; a squirrel springs playfully across the road, and up into the tree; we cast our eye searchingly over the wood-grown mountain-side, which slopes so far, far forward; but not a trace of a house is to be seen: no-where does that blueish smoke-cloud rise, that shows us, here are fellow-men.

The sun shines warm; the flies dance around the horses, set-tle on them, fly off again, and dance, as though it were to qualify themselves for resting and being still. They perhaps think: "Nothing is going on without us: there is no life while we are doing noth-ing." They think, as many persons think, and do not remember that Time's horses always fly onward with us!

How solitary it is here!—so delightfully solitary! one is so entirely alone with God and one's self. As the sunlight streams forth over the earth, and over the extensive solitary forests, so does God's spirit stream over and into mankind; ideas and thoughts unfold themselves—endless, inexhaustible, as he is—as the mag-net which apportions its powers to the steel, and itself loses noth-ing thereby. As our journey through the forest-scenery here along the extended solitary road, so, travelling on the great high-road of thought, ideas pass through our head. Strange, rich caravans pass by from the works of poets, from the home of memory, strange and novel—for capricious fancy gives birth to them at the moment. There comes a procession of pious children with waving flags and joyous songs; there come dancing Moenades, the blood's wild Bac-chantes. The sun pours down hot in the open forest: it is as if the Southern summer had laid itself up here to rest in Scandinavian forest-solitude, and sought itself out a glade where it might lie in the sun's hot beams and sleep: hence this stillness, as if it were night. Not a bird is heard to twitter, not a pine-tree moves: of what does the Southern summer dream here in the North, amongst pines and fragrant birches?

In the writings of the olden time, from the classic soil of the South, are *sagas* of mighty fairies who, in the skins of swans, flew towards the North, to the Hyperborean's land, to the east of the north wind; up there, in the deep, still lakes, they bathed themselves, and acquired a renewed form. We are in the forest by these deep lakes; we see swans in flocks fly over us, and swim upon the rapid elv and on the still waters. The forests, we perceive, continue to extend further towards the west and the north, and are more dense as we proceed: the carriage-roads cease, and one can only pursue one's way along the outskirts by the solitary path, and on horseback.

The saga, from the time of the plague (A.D., 1350), here impresses itself on the mind, when the pestilence passed through the land, and transformed cultivated fields and towns—nay, whole parishes, into barren fields and wild forests. Deserted and forgotten, overgrown with moss, grass, and bushes, churches stood for years far in the forest; no one knew of their existence, until, in a later century, a huntsman lost himself here: his arrow rebounded from the green wall, the moss of which he loosened, and the church was found. The wood-cutter felled the trees for fuel; his axe struck against the overgrown wall, and it gave way to the blow; the fir-planks fell, and the church, from the time of the pestilence, was discovered; the sun again shone bright through the openings of the doors and windows, on the brass candelabra and the altar, where the communion-cup still stood. The cuckoo came, sat there, and sang: "Many, many years shalt thou live!"

Woodland solitude! what images dost thou not present to our thoughts! Woodland solitude! through thy vaulted halls people now pass in the summer-time with cattle and domestic utensils; children and old men go to the solitary pasture where echo dwells, where the national song springs forth with the wild mountain flower! Dost thou see the procession?—paint it if thou canst! The broad wooden cart laden high with chests and barrels, with jars and with crockery. The bright copper kettle and the tin dish shine in the sun. The old grandmother sits at the top of the load and holds her spinning-wheel, which completes the pyramid. The father drives the horse, the mother carries the youngest child on her back, sewed up in a skin, and the procession moves on step by step. The cattle are driven by the half-grown children: they have stuck a birch branch between one of the cows' horns, but she does not appear to be proud of her finery, she goes the same quiet pace as the others and lashes the saucy flies with her tail. If the night becomes cold on this solitary pasture, there is fuel enough here—the tree falls of itself from old age and lies and rots.

But take especial care of the fire fear the fire-spirit in the forest desert! He comes from the unextinguishable pile—he comes from the thunder-cloud, riding on the blue lightning's flame, which kindles the thick, dry moss of the earth: trees and bushes are kindled, the flames run from tree to tree—it is like a snow-storm of fire! the flame leaps to the tops of the trees—what a crackling and roaring, as if it were the ocean in its course! The birds fly upward in flocks, and fall down suffocated by the smoke; the animals flee, or, encircled by the fire, are consumed in it! Hear their cries and roars of agony! The howling of the wolf and the bear, dos't thou know it? A calm, rainy-day, and the forest-plains themselves, alone are able to confine the fiery sea, and the burnt forest stands charred, with black trunks and black stumps of trees, as we saw them here in the forest by the broad high-road. On this road we continue to travel, but it becomes worse and worse; it is, properly speaking, no road at all, but it is about to become one. Large stones lie half dug up, and we drive past them; large trees are cast down, and obstruct our way, and therefore we must descend from the carriage. The horses are taken out, and the peasants help to lift and push the carriage forward over ditches and opened paths.

The sun now ceases to shine; some few rain-drops fall, and now it is a steady rain. But how it causes the birch to shed its fragrance! At a distance there are huts erected, of loose trunks of trees and fresh green boughs, and in each there is a large fire burning. See where the blue smoke curls through the green leafy roof; peasants are within at work, hammering and forging; here they have their meals. They are now laying a mine in order to blast a rock, and the rain falls faster and faster, and the pine and birch emit a finer fragrance. It is delightful in the forest.

FAHLUN

꧁꧂

We made our way at length out of the forest, and saw a town before us enveloped in thick smoke, having a similar appearance to most of the English manufacturing towns, save that the smoke was greenish—it was the town Fahlun.

The road now went downwards between large banks, formed by the dross deposited here from the smelting furnaces, and which looks like burnt-out hardened lava. No sprout or shrub was to be seen, not a blade of grass peeped forth by the way-side, not a bird flew past, but a strong sulphurous smell, as from among the craters in Solfatara, filled the air. The copper roof of the church shone with corrosive green.

Long straight streets now appeared in view. It was as deathly still here as if sickness and disease had lain within these dark wooden houses, and frightened the inhabitants from coming abroad; yet sickness and disease come but to few here, for when the plague raged in Sweden, the rich and powerful of the land hastened to Fahlun, whose sulphureous air was the most healthy. An ochre-yellow water runs through the brook, between the houses; the smoke from the mines and smelting furnaces has imparted its tinge to them; it has even penetrated into the church, whose slender pillars are dark from the fumes of the copper. There chanced to come on a thunder-storm when we arrived, but its roaring and the lightning's flashes harmonized well with this town, which appears as if it were built on the edge of a crater.

We went to see the copper mine which gives the whole district the name of "Stora Kopparberget," (the great copper mountain). According to the legend, its riches were discovered by two goats which were fighting—they struck the ground with their horns and some copper ore adhered to them.

From the solitary red-ochre street we wandered over the great heaps of burnt-out dross and fragments of stone, accumulated to whole ramparts and hills. The fire shone from the smelting furnaces with green, yellow and red tongues of flame under a blue-green smoke; half-naked, black-smeared fellows threw out large glowing masses of fire, so that the sparks flew around and about:—one was reminded of Schiller's "Fridolin."

The thick sulphureous smoke poured forth from the heaps of cleansed ore, under which the fire was in full activity, and the wind drove it across the road which we must pass. In smoke, and impregnated with smoke, stood building after building: three buildings had been strangely thrown, as it were, by one another: earth and stone-heaps, as if they were unfinished works of defence, extended around. Scaffolding, and long wooden bridges, had been erected there; large wheels turned round; long and heavy iron chains were in continual motion.

We stood before an immense gulf, called "Stora Stoeten," (the great mine). It had formerly three entrances, but they fell in and now there is but one. This immense sunken gulf now appears like a vast valley: the many openings below, to the shafts of the mine, look, from above, like the sand-martin's dark nest-holes in the declivities of the shore: there were a few wooden huts down there. Some strangers in miners' dresses, with their guide, each carrying a lighted fir-torch, appeared at the bottom, and disappeared again in one of the dark holes. From within the dark wooden houses, in which great water-wheels turned, issued some of the workmen. They came from the dizzying gulf—from narrow, deep wells: they stood in their wooden shoes two and two, on the edge of the tun which, attached to heavy chains, is hoisted up, singing and swinging the tun on all sides: they came up merry enough. Habit makes one daring.

They told us that, during the passage upwards, it often happened that one or another, from pure wantonness, stepped quite out of the tun, and sat himself between the loose stones on the projecting piece of rock, whilst they fired and blasted the rock below so that it shook again, and the stones about him thundered down. Should one expostulate with him on his fool-hardiness, he would answer with the usual witticism here: "I have never before killed myself."

One descends into some of the shafts by a sort of machinery, which looks as if they had placed two iron ladders against each other, each having a rocking movement, so that by treading on the ascending-step on the one side and then on the other, which goes upwards, one gradually ascends, and by going on the downward sinking-step one gets by degrees to the bottom. They said it was very easy, only one must step boldly, so that the foot should not come between and get crushed; and then one must remember that there is no railing or balustrade here, and directly outside these stairs there is the deep abyss into which one may fall headlong. The deepest shaft has a perpendicular depth of more than a hundred and ninety fathoms, but for this there is no danger, they say, only one must not be dizzy, nor get alarmed. One of the workmen, who had come up, descended with a lighted pine-branch as a torch: the flame illumined the dark rocky wall, and by degrees became only a faint streak of light which soon vanished.

We were told that a few days before, five or six schoolboys had unobserved stolen in here, and amused themselves by going from step to step on these machine-like rocking stairs, in pitchy darkness, but at last they knew not rightly which way to go, up or down, and had then begun to shout and scream lustily. They escaped luckily that bout.

By one of the large openings, called "Fat Mads," there are rich copper mines, but which have not yet been worked. A building stands above it: it was at the bottom of this that they found, in the year 1719, the corpse of a young miner. It appeared as if he had fallen down that very day, so unchanged did the body seem— but no one knew him. An old woman then stepped forward and burst into tears: the deceased was her bridegroom, who had disappeared forty nine years ago. She stood there old and wrinkled; he was young as when they had met for the last time nearly half a century before.[t]

---

t   In another mine they found, in the year 1635, a corpse perfectly fresh, and almost with the appearance of one asleep; but his clothes, and the ancient copper coins found on him, bore witness that it was two hundred years since he had perished there.

We went to "The Plant House," as it is called, where the vitriolated liquid is crystallized to sulphate of copper. It grew up long sticks placed upright in the boiling water, resembling long pieces of grass-green sugar. The steam was pungent, and the air in here penetrated our tongues—it was just as if one had a corroded spoon in one's mouth. It was really a luxury to come out again, even into the rarefied copper smoke, under the open sky.

Steaming, burnt-out, and herbless as the district is on this side of the town, it is just as refreshing, green, and fertile on the opposite side of Fahlun. Tall leafy trees grow close to the farthest houses. One is directly in the fresh pine and birch forests, thence to the lake and to the distant blueish mountain sides near Zaether.

The people here can tell you and show you memorials of Engelbrekt and his Dalecarlians' deeds, and of Gustavus Vasa's adventurous wanderings. But we will remain here in this smoke-enveloped town, with the silent street's dark houses. It was almost midnight when we went out and came to the market-place. There was a wedding in one of the houses, and a great crowd of persons stood outside, the women nearest the house, the men a little further back. According to an old Swedish custom, they called for the bride and bridegroom to come forward, and they did so—they durst not do otherwise. Peasant girls, with candles in their hands, stood on each side; it was a perfect tableau: the bride with downcast eyes, the bridegroom smiling, and the young bridesmaids each with a laughing face. And the people shouted: "Now turn yourselves a little! now the back! now the face! the bridegroom quite round, the bride a little nearer!" And the bridal pair turned and turned—nor was criticism wanting. In this instance, however, it was to their praise and honour, but that is not always the case. It may be a painful and terrible hour for a newly-wedded pair: if they do not please the public, or if they have something to say against the match, or the persons themselves, they are then soon made to know what is thought of them. There is perhaps also heard some rude jest or another, accompanied by the laughter of the crowd. We were told, that even in Stockholm the same custom was observed among the lower classes until a few years ago, so that a bridal pair, who, in order to avoid this exposure, wanted to drive off, were stopped by the crowd, the carriage-door was opened on each side, and the whole public marched through the carriage. They would see the bride and bridegroom—that was their right.

Here, in Fahlun, the exhibition was friendly; the bridal pair smiled, the bridesmaids also, and the assembled crowd laughed and shouted, hurra! In the rest of the market-place and the streets around, there was dead silence and solitude.

The roseate hue of eve still shone: it passed, changed into that of morn—it was the Midsummer time.

What the Straws Said

On the lake there glided a boat, and the party within it sang Swedish and Danish songs; but by the shore, under that tall, hanging birch, sat four young girls—so pretty—so sylph-like! and they each plucked up from the grass four long straws, and bound these straws two and two together, at the top and the bottom.

"We shall now see if they will come together in a square," said the girls: "if it be so, then that which I think of will be fulfilled," and they bound them, and they thought.

No one got to know the secret thought, the heart's silent wish of the others. But yet a little bird sings about it.

The thoughts of one flew over sea and land, over the high mountains, where the mule finds its way in the mists, down to Mignon's beautiful land, where the old gods live in marble and painting. "Thither, thither! shall I ever get there?" That was the wish, that was the thought, and she opened her hand, looked at the bound straws, and they appeared only two and two bound together.

And where were the second one's thoughts? also in foreign lands, in the gunpowder's smoke, amongst the glitter of arms and cannons, with him, the friend of her childhood, fighting for imperial power, against the Hungarian people. Will he return joyful and unharmed—return to Sweden's peaceful, well-constituted, happy land? The straws showed no square: a tear dwelt in the girl's eye.

The third smiled: there was a sort of mischief in the smile. Will our aged bachelor and that old maiden-lady yonder, who now wander along so young, smile so young, and speak so youthfully to each other, not be a married couple before the cuckoo sings again next year? See—that is what I should like to know! and the smile played around the thinker's mouth, but she did not speak her thoughts. The straws were separated—consequently the bachelor and the old maid also. "It may, however, happen nevertheless," she certainly thought: it was apparent in the smile; it was obvious in the manner in which she threw the straws away.

"There is nothing I would know—nothing that I am curious to know!" said the fourth; but yet she bound the straws together; for within her also there was a wish alive; but no bird has sung about it; no one guesses it.

Rock thyself securely in the heart's lotus flower, thou shining humming-bird, thy' name shall not be pronounced: and besides the straws said as before—"without hope!"

"Now you! now you!" cried the young girls to a stranger, far from the neighbouring land, from the green isle, that Gylfe ploughed from Sweden. "What dear thing do you wish shall happen, or not happen!—tell us the wish!"—"If the oracle speaks well for me," said he, "then I will tell you the silent wish and prayer, with which I bind these knots on the grass straw; but if I have no better success than you have had, I will then be silent!" and he bound straw to straw, and as he bound, he repeated: "it signifies nothing!" He now opened his hand, his eyes shone brighter, his heart beat faster. The straws formed a square! "It will happen, it will happen!" cried the young girls. "What did you wish for?" "That Denmark may soon gain an honourable peace!"

"It will happen! it will happen!" said the young girls; "and when it happens, we will remember that the straws have told it before-hand."

"I will keep these four straws, bound in a prophetic wreath for victory and peace!" said the stranger; "and if the oracle speaks truth, then I will draw the whole picture for you, as we sit here under the hanging birch by the lake, and look on Zaether's blue mountains, each of us binding straw to straw."

A red mark was made in the almanack; it was the 6th of July, 1849. The same day a red page was written in Denmark's history. The Danish soldier made a red, victorious mark with his blood, at the battle of Fredericia.

THE POET'S SYMBOL

If a man would seek for the symbol of the poet, he need not look farther than "The Arabian Nights' Tales." Scherezade who interprets the stories for the Sultan—Scherezade is the poet, and the Sultan is the public who is to be agreeably entertained, or else he will decapitate Scherezade.

Powerful Sultan! Poor Scherezade!

The Sultan-public sits in more than a thousand and one forms, and listens. Let us regard a few of these forms.

There sits a sallow, peevish, scholar; the tree of his life bears leaves impressed with long and learned words: diligence and perseverance crawl like snails on the hog's leather bark: the moths have got into the inside—and that is bad, very bad! Pardon the rich fulness of the song, the inconsiderate enthusiasm, the fresh young, intellect. Do not behead Scherezade! But he beheads her out of hand, *sans* remorse.

There sits a dress-maker, a sempstress who has had some experience of the world. She comes from strange families, from a solitary chamber where she sat and gained a knowledge of mankind—she knows and loves the romantic. Pardon, Miss, if the story has not excitement enough for you, who have sat over the needle and the muslin, and having had so much of life's prose, gasp after romance.

"Behead her!" says the dress-maker.

There sits a figure in a dressing gown—this oriental dress of the North, for the lordly minion, the petty prince, the rich brewer's son, &c., &c., &c. It is not to be learned from the dressing gown, nor from that lordly look and the fine smile around the mouth, to what stem he belongs: his demands on Scherezade are just the same as the dress-maker's: he must be excited, he must be brought to shudder all down the vertebrae, through the very spine: he must be crammed with mys-teries, such as those which Spriez knew how to connect and thicken.

Scherezade is beheaded!

Wise, enlightened Sultan! Thou comest in the form of a school-boy; thou bearest the Romans and Greeks together in a satchel on thy back, as Atlas sustained the world. Do not cast an evil eye upon poor Scherezade; do not judge her before thou hast learned thy les-son, and art a child again,—do not behead Scherezade!

Young, full-dressed diplomatist, on whose breast we can count, by the badges of honour, how many courts thou hast visited with thy princely master, speak mildly of Scherezade's name! speak of her in French, that she may be ennobled above her mother tongue! trans-late but one strophe of her song, as badly as thou canst, but carry it into the brilliant saloon, and her sentence of death is annulled in the sweet, absolving *charmant!*

Mighty annihilator and elevator!—the newspapers' Zeus—thou weekly, monthly, and daily journals' Jupiter, shake not thy locks in anger! Cast not thy lightnings forth, if Scherezade sing otherwise than thou art accustomed to in thy family, or if she go without a *suite* of thine own clique. Do not behead her!

We will see one figure more—the most dangerous of them all; he with the praise on his lips, like that of the stormy river's swell— the blind enthusiast. The water in which Scherezade dipped her fin-gers, is for him a fountain of Castalia; the throne he erects to her apotheosis becomes her scaffold.

This is the poet's symbol—paint it:

"THE SULTAN AND SCHEREZADE."

But why none of the worthier figures—the candid, the honest, and the beautiful? They come also, and on them Scherezade fixes her eye. Encouraged by them, she boldly raises her proud head aloft towards the stars, and sings of the harmony there above, and here beneath, in man's heart.

That will not clearly show the symbol:

"THE SULTAN AND SCHEREZADE."

The sword of death hangs over her head whilst she relates—and the Sultan-figure bids us expect that it will fall. Scherezade is the victor: the poet is, like her, also a victor. He is rich, victorious—even in his poor chamber, in his most solitary hours. There, in that chamber, rose after rose shoots forth; bubble after bubble sparkles on the magic stream. The heavens shine with shooting stars, as if a new firmament were created, and the old rolled away. The world does not know it, for it is the poet's own creation, richer than the king's costly illuminations. He is happy, as Scherezade is; he is victorious, he is mighty. *Imagination* adorns his walls with tapestry, such as no land's ruler owns; *feeling* makes the beauteous chords sound to him from the human breast; *understanding* raises him, through the magnificence of creation, up to God, without his forgetting that he stands fast on the firm earth. He is mighty, he is happy, as few are. We will not place him in the stocks of misconstruction, for pity and lamentation; we merely paint his symbol, dip into the colours on the world's least attractive side, and obtain it most comprehensibly from

"THE SULTAN AND SCHEREZADE."

See—that is it! Do not behead Scherezade!

THE DAL-ELV

B efore Homer sang there were heroes; but they are not known; no poet celebrated their fame. It is just so with the beauties of nature, they must be brought into notice by words and delineations, be brought before the eyes of the multitude; get a sort of world's patent for what they are, and then they may be said first to exist. The elvs of the north have rushed and whirled along for thousands of years in unknown beauty. The world's great highroad does take this direction; no steam-packet conveys the traveller comfortably along the streams of the Dal-elvs; fall on fall makes sluices indispensable and invaluable. Schubert is as yet the only stranger who has written about the wild magnificence and southern beauty of Dalecarlia, and spoken of its greatness.

Clear as the waves of the sea does the mighty elv stream in endless windings through forest deserts and varying plains, sometimes extending its deep bed, sometimes confining it, reflecting the bending trees and the red painted block houses of solitary towns, and sometimes rushing like a cataract over immense blocks of rock.

Miles apart from one another, out of the ridge of mountains between Sweden and Norway, come the east and west Dal-elvs, which first become confluent and have one bed above Balstad. They have taken up rivers and lakes in their waters. Do but visit this place! here are pictorial riches to be found; the most picturesque landscapes, dizzyingly grand, smilingly pastoral—idyllic: one is drawn onward up to the very source of the elv, the bubbling well above Finman's hut: one feels a desire to follow every branch of the stream that the river takes in.

The first mighty fall, Njupeskoers cataract, is seen by the Norwegian frontier in Sernasog. The mountain stream rushes perpendicularly from the rock to a depth of seventy fathoms.

We pause in the dark forest, where the elv seems to collect within itself nature's whole deep gravity. The stream rolls its clear waters over a porphyry soil where the mill-wheel is driven, and the gigantic porphyry bowls and sarcophagi are polished.

We follow the stream through Siljan's lake, where superstition sees the water-sprite swim, like the sea-horse with a mane of green sea-weed, and where the aerial images present visions of witchcraft in the warm summer days.

We sail on the stream from Siljan's lake, under the weeping willows of the parsonage, where the swans assemble in flocks; we glide along slowly with horses and carriages on the great ferry-boat, away over the rapid current under Balstad's picturesque shore. Here the elv widens and rolls its billows majestically in a woodland landscape, as large and extended as if it were in North America.

We see the rushing, rapid stream under Avista's yellow clay declivities: the yellow water falls like fluid amber in picturesque cataracts before the copper-works, where rainbow-coloured tongues of fire shoot themselves upwards, and the hammer's blows on the copper plates resound to the monotonous, roaring rumble of the elv-fall.

And now, as a concluding passage of splendour in the life of the Dal-elvs, before they lose themselves in the waters of the Baltic, is the view of Elvkarleby Fall. Schubert compares it with the fall of Schafhausen; but we must remember, that the Rhine there has not such a mass of water as that which rushes down Elvkarleby.

Two and a half Swedish miles from Gefle, where the high road to Upsala goes over the Dal-elv, we see from the walled bridge, which we pass over, the whole of that immense fall. Close up to the bridge, there is a house where the bridge toll is paid. There the stranger can pass the night, and from his little window look over the falling waters, see them in the clear moonlight, when darkness has laid itself to rest within the thicket of oaks and firs, and all the effect of light is in those foaming, flowing waters, and see them when the morning sun stretches his rainbow in the trembling spray, like an airy bridge of colours, from the shore to the wood-grown rock in the centre of the cataract.

We came hither from Gefle, and saw at a great distance on the way, the blue clouds from the broken, rising spray, ascend above the dark-green tops of the trees. The carriage stopped near the bridge; we stepped out, and close before us fell the whole redundant elv.

The painter cannot give us the true, living image of a waterfall on canvas—the movement is wanting; how can one describe it in words, delineate this majestic grandeur, brilliancy of colour, and arrowy flight? One cannot do it; one may however attempt it; get together, by little and little, with words, an outline of that mirrored image which our eye gave us, and which even the strongest remembrance can only retain—if not vaguely, dubiously.

The Dal-elv divides itself into three branches above the fall: the two enclose a wood-grown rocky island, and rush down round its smooth-worn stony wall. The one to the right of these two falls is the finer; the third branch makes a circuit, and comes again to the main stream, close outside the united fall; here it dashes out as if to meet or stop the others, and is now hurried along in boiling eddies with the arrowy stream, which rushes on foaming against the walled pillars that bear the bridge, as if it would tear them away along with it.

The landscape to the left was enlivened by a herd of goats, that were browsing amongst the hazel bushes. They ventured quite out to the very edge of the declivity, as they were bred here and accustomed to the hollow, thundering rumble of the water. To the right, a flock of screaming birds flew over the magnificent oaks. Cars, each with one horse, and with the driver standing upright in it, the reins in his hand, came on the broad forest road from Oens Brueck.

Thither we will go in order to take leave of the Dal-elv at one of the most delightful of places, which vividly removes the stranger, as it were, into a far more southern land, into a far richer nature, than he supposed was to be found here. The road is so pretty—the oak grows here so strong and vigorously with mighty crowns of rich foliage.

Oens Brueck lies in a delightfully pastoral situation. We came thither; here was life and bustle indeed! The mill-wheels went round; large beams were sawn through; the iron forged on the anvil, and all by water-power. The houses of the workmen form a whole town: it is a long street with red-painted wooden houses, under picturesque oaks, and birch trees. The greensward was as soft as velvet to look at, and up at the manor-house, which rises in front of the garden like a little palace, there was, in the rooms and saloon, everything that the English call comfort.

We did not find the host at home; but hospitality is always the house-fairy here. We had everything good and homely. Fish and wild fowl were placed before us, steaming and fragrant, and almost as quickly as in beautiful enchanted palaces. The garden itself was a piece of enchantment. Here stood three transplanted beech-trees, and they throve well. The sharp north wind had rounded off the tops of the wild chestnut-trees of the avenue in a singular manner: they looked as if they had been under the gardener's shears. Golden-yellow oranges hung in the conservatory; the splendid southern exotics had to-day got the windows half open, so that the artificial warmth met the fresh, warm, sunny air of the northern summer.

That branch of the Dal-elv which goes round the garden is strewn with small islands, where beautiful hanging birches and fir-trees grow in Scandinavian splendour. There are small islands with green, silent groves; there are small islands with rich grass, tall brackens, variegated bell-flowers, and cowslips—no Turkey carpet has fresher colours. The stream between these islands and holms is sometimes rapid, deep, and clear; sometimes like a broad rivulet with silky-green rushes, water-lilies, and brown-feathered reeds; sometimes it is a brook with a stony ground, and now it spreads itself out in a large, still mill-dam.

Here is a landscape in Midsummer for the games of the river-sprites, and the dancers of the elves and fairies! Here, in the lustre of the full moon, the dryads can tell their tales, the water-sprite seize the golden harp, and believe that one can be blessed, at least for one single night like this.

On the other side of Oens Brueck is the main stream—the full Dal-elv. Do you hear the monotonous rumble? it is not from Elvkarleby Fall that it reaches hither; it is close by; it is from Laa-

Foss, in which lies Ash Island: the elv streams and rushes over the leaping salmon.

Let us sit here, between the fragments of rock by the shore, in the red evening sunlight, which sheds a golden lustre on the waters of the Dal-elv.

Glorious river! But a few seconds' work hast thou to do in the mills yonder, and thou rushest foaming on over Elvkarleby's rocks, down into the deep bed of the river, which leads thee to the Baltic—thy eternity.

DANEMORA

⁂

Reader, do you know what giddiness is? Pray that she may not seize you, this mighty "Loreley" of the heights, this evil-genius from the land of the sylphides; she whizzes around her prey, and whirls it into the abyss. She sits on the narrow rocky path, close by the steep declivity, where no tree, no branch is found, where the wanderer must creep close to the side of the rock, and look steadily forward. She sits on the church spire and nods to the plumber who works on his swaying scaffold; she glides into the illumined saloon, and up to the nervous, solitary one, in the middle of the bright polished floor, and it sways under him—the walls vanish from him.

Her fingers touch one of the hairs of our head, and we feel as if the air had left us, and we were in a vacuum.

We met with her at Danemora's immense gulf, whither we came on broad, smooth, excellent high-roads, through the fresh forest. She sat on the extreme edge of the rocky wall, above the abyss, and kicked at the tun with her thin, awl-like legs, as it hung in iron chains on large beams, from the tower-high corner of the bridge by the precipice.

The traveller raised his foot over the abyss, and set it on the tun, into which one of the workmen received him, and held him; and the chains rattled; the pulleys turned; the tun sank slowly, hovering through the air. But he felt the descent; he felt it through his bones and marrow; through all the nerves. Her icy breath blew in his neck, and down the spine, and the air itself became colder and colder. It seemed to him as if the rocks grew over his head, always higher and higher: the tun made a slight swinging, but he felt it, like a fall—a fall in sleep, that shock in the blood. Did it go quicker downwards, or was it going up again? He could not distinguish by the sensation.

The tun touched the ground, or rather the snow—the dirty trodden, eternal snow, down to which no sunbeam reaches, which no summer warmth from above ever melts. A hollow sound was heard from within the dark, yawning cavern, and a thick vapour rolled out into the cold air. The stranger entered the dark halls; there seemed to be a crashing above him: the fire burned; the furnaces roared; the beating of hammers sounded; the watery damps dripped down—and he again entered the tun, which was hoven up in the air. He sat with closed eyes, but giddiness breathed on his head, and on his breast; his inwardly-turned eye measured the giddy depth through the tun: "It is appalling," said he.

"Appalling!" echoed the brave and estimable stranger, whom we met at Danemora's great gulf. He was a man from Scania, consequently from the same street as the Sealander—if the Sound be called a street (strait). "But, however, one can say one has been down there," said he, and he pointed to the gulf; "right down, and up again; but it is no pleasure at all."

"But why descend at all?" said I. "Why will men do these things?"

"One must, you know, when one comes here," said he. "The plague of travelling is, that one must see everything: one would not have it supposed otherwise. It is a shame to a man, when he gets home again, not to have seen everything, that others ask him about."

"If you have no desire, then let it alone. See what pleases you on your travels. Go two paces nearer than where you stand, and become quite giddy: you will then have formed some conception of the passage downward. I will hold you fast, and describe the rest of it for you." And I did so, and the perspiration sprang from his forehead.

"Yes, so it is: I apprehend it all," said he: "I am clearly sensible of it."

I described the dirty grey snow covering, which the sun's warmth never thaws; the cold down there, and the caverns, and the fire, and the workmen, &c.

"Yes; one should be able to tell all about it," said he. "That *you* can, for you have seen it."

"No more than you," said I. "I came to the gulf; I saw the depth, the snow below, the smoke that rolled out of the caverns; but when it was time I should get into the tun—no, thank you. Giddiness tickled me with her long, awl-like legs, and so I stayed where I was I have felt the descent, through the spine and the soles of the feet, and that as well as any one: the descent is the pinch. I have been in the Hartz, under Rammelsberg; glided, as on Russian mountains, at Hallein, through the mountain, from the top down to the salt-works; wandered about in the catacombs of Rome and Malta: and what does one see in the deep passages? Gloom—darkness! What does one feel? Cold, and a sense of oppression—a longing for air and light, which is by far the best; and that we have now."

"But nevertheless, it is so very remarkable!" said the man; and he drew forth his "Hand-book for Travellers in Sweden," from which he read: "Danemora's iron-works are the oldest, largest, and richest in Sweden; the best in Europe. They have seventy-nine openings, of which seventeen only are being worked. The machine mine is ninety-three fathoms deep."

Just then the bells sounded from below: it was the signal that the time of labour for that day was ended. The hue of eve still shone on the tops of the trees above; but down in that deep, far-extended gulf, it was a perfect twilight. Thence, and out of the dark caverns, the workmen swarmed forth. They looked like flies, quite small in the space below: they scrambled up the long ladders, which hung from the steep sides of the rocks, in separate landing-places: they climbed higher and higher—upwards, upwards—and at every step they became larger. The iron chains creaked in the scaffolding of beams, and three or four young fellows stood in their wooden shoes on the edge of the tun; chatted away right merrily, and kicked with their feet against the side of the rock, so that they swung from it: and it became darker and darker below; it was as if the deep abyss became still deeper!

"It is appalling!" said the man from Scania. "One ought, however, to have gone down there, if it were only to swear that one *had* been. You, however, have certainly been down there," said he again to me.

"Believe what you will," I replied; and I say the same to the reader.

THE SWINE

That capital fellow, Charles Dickens, has told us about the swine, and since then it puts us into a good humour whenever we hear even the grunt of one. Saint Anthony has taken them under his patronage, and if we think of the "prodigal son," we are at once in the midst of the sty, and it was just before such a one that our carriage stopped in Sweden. By the high road, closely adjoining his house, the peasant had his sty, and that such a one as there is probably scarcely its like in the world. It was an old state-carriage, the seats were taken out of it, the wheels taken off, and thus it stood, without further ceremony, on its own bottom, and four swine were shut in there. If these were the first that had been in it one could not determine; but that it was once a state-carriage everything about it bore witness, even to the strip of morocco that hung from the roof inside, all bore witness of better days. It is true, every word of it.

"Uff," said the occupiers within, and the carriage creaked and complained—it was a sorrowful end it had come to.

"The beautiful is past!" so it sighed; so it said, or it might have said so.

We returned here in the autumn. The carriage, or rather the body of the carriage, stood in its old place, but the swine were gone: they were lords in the forests; rain and drizzle reigned there; the wind tore the leaves off all the trees, and allowed them neither rest nor quiet: the birds of passage were gone.

"The beautiful is past!" said the carriage, and the same sigh passed through the whole of nature, and from the human heart it sounded: "The beautiful is past! with the delightful green forest, with the warm sunshine, and the song of birds—past! past!" So it said, and so it creaked in the trunks of the tall trees, and there was heard a sigh, so inwardly deep, a sigh direct from the heart of the wild rose-bush, and he who sat there was the rose-king. Do you know him! he is of a pure breed, the finest red-green breed: he is easily known. Go to the wild rose hedges, and in autumn, when all the flowers are gone, and the red hips alone remain, one often sees amongst these a large red-green moss-flower: that is the rose-king. A little green leaf grows out of his head—that is his feather: he is the only male person of his kind on the rose-bush, and he it was who sighed.

"Past! past! the beautiful is past! The roses are gone; the leaves of the trees fall off!—it is wet here, and it is cold and raw!—The birds that sang here are now silent; the swine live on acorns; the swine are lords in the forest!"

They were cold nights, they were gloomy days; but the raven sat on the bough and croaked nevertheless: "brah, brah!" The raven and the crow sat on the topmost bough: they have a large family, and they all said: "brah, brah! caw, caw!" and the majority is always right.

There was a great miry pool under the tall trees in the hollow, and here lay the whole herd of swine, great and small—they found the place so excellent. "Oui! oui!" said they, for they knew no more French, but that, however, was something. They were so wise, and so fat, and altogether lords in the forest.

The old ones lay still, for they thought; the young ones, on the contrary, were so brisk—busy, but apparently uneasy. One little pig had a curly tail—that curl was the mother's delight. She thought that they all looked at the curl, and thought only of the curl; but that they did not. They thought of themselves, and of what was useful, and of what the forest was for. They had always heard that the acorns they ate grew on the roots of the trees, and therefore they had always rooted there; but now there came a little one—for it is always the young ones that come with news—and he asserted that the acorns fell down from the branches: he himself had felt one fall right on his head, and that had given him the idea, so he had made observations, and now he was quite sure of what he asserted. The old ones laid their heads together. "Uff," said the swine, "uff! the finery is past! the twittering of the birds is past! we will have fruit! whatever can be eaten is good, and we eat everything!"

"Oui! oui!" said they altogether.

But the mother sow looked at her little pig with the curly tail.

"One must not, however, forget the beautiful!" said she.

"Caw! caw!" screamed the crow, and flew down, in order to be appointed nightingale: one there should be—and so the crow was directly appointed.

"Past! past!" sighed the Rose King, "all the beautiful is past!"

It was wet; it was gloomy; there was cold and wind, and the rain pelted down over the fields, and through the forest, like long water jets. Where are the birds that sang? where are the flowers in the meadows, and the sweet berries in the wood?—past! past!

A light shone from the forester's house: it twinkled like a star, and shed its long rays out between the trees. A song was heard from within; pretty children played around their old grandfather, who sat with the Bible on his lap and read about God, and eternal life, and spoke of the spring that would come again: he spoke of the forest that would renew its green leaves, of the roses that would flower, of the nightingales that would sing, and of the beautiful that would again be paramount.

But the Rose King did not hear it; he sat in the raw, cold weather, and sighed:

"Past! past!"

And the swine were lords in the forest, and the mother sow looked at her little pig, and his curly tail.

"There will always be some, who have a sense for the beautiful!" said the mother sow.

Poetry's California

Nature's treasures are most often unveiled to us by accident. A dog's nose was dyed by the bruised purple fish, and the genuine purple dye was discovered; a pair of wild buffalos were fighting on America's auriferous soil, and their horns tore up the green sward that covered the rich gold vein.

"In former days," as it is said by most, "everything came spontaneously. Our age has not such revelations; now one must slave and drudge if one would get anything; one must dig down into the deep shafts after the metals, which decrease more and more;—when the earth suddenly stretches forth her golden finger from California's peninsula, and we there see Monte Christo's foolishly invented riches realized; we see Aladdin's cave with its inestimable treasures. The world's treasury is so endlessly rich that we have, to speak plain and straightforward, scraped a little off the up-heaped measure; but the bushel is still full, the whole of the real measure is now refilled. In science also, such a world lies open for the discoveries of the human mind!

"But in poetry, the greatest and most glorious is already found, and gained!" says the poet. "Happy he who was born in former times; there was then many a land still undiscovered, on which poetry's rich gold lay like the ore that shines forth from the earth's surface."

Do not speak so! happy poet thou, who art born in our time! thou dost inherit all the glorious treasures which thy predecessors gave to the world; thou dost learn from them, that truth only is eternal,—the true in nature and mankind.

Our time is the time of discoveries—poetry also has its new California.

"Where does it exist?" you ask.

The coast is so near, that you do not think that *there* is the new world. Like a bold Leander, swim with me across the stream: the black words on the white paper will waft you—every period is a heave of the waves.

✣

It was in the library's saloon. Book-shelves with many books, old and new, were ranged around for every one; manuscripts lay there in heaps; there were also maps and globes. There sat industrious men at little tables, and wrote out and wrote in, and that was no easy work. But suddenly, a great transformation took place; the shelves became terraces for the noblest trees, with flowers and fruit; heavy clusters of grapes hung amongst leafy vines, and there was life and movement all around.

The old folios and dusty manuscripts rose into flower-covered tumuli, and there sprang forth knights in mail, and kings with golden crowns on, and there was the clang of harp and shield; history acquired the life and fullness of poetry—for a poet had entered there. He saw the living visions; breathed the flowers' fragrance; crushed the grapes, and drank the sacred juice. But he himself knew not yet that he was a poet—the bearer of-light for times and generations yet to come.

It was in the fresh, fragrant forest, in the last hour of leave-taking. Love's kiss, as the farewell, was the initiatory baptism for the future poetic life; and the fresh fragrance of the forest became sweeter, the chirping of the birds more melodious: there came sunlight and cooling breezes. Nature becomes doubly delightful where a poet walks.

And as there were two roads before Hercules, so there were before him two roads, shown by two figures, in order to serve him; the one an old crone, the other a youth, beautiful as the angel that led the young Tobias.

The old crone had on a mantle, on which were wrought flowers, animals, and human beings, entwined in an arabesque manner. She had large spectacles on, and beside her lantern she held a bag filled with old gilt cards—apparatus for witchcraft, and all the amulets of superstition: leaning on her crutch, wrinkled and shivering, she was, however, soaring, like the mist over the meadow.

"Come with me, and you shall see the world, so that a poet can have benefit from it," said she. "I will light my lantern; it is better than that which Diogenes bore; I shall lighten your path."

And the light shone; the old crone lifted her head, and stood there strong and tall, a powerful female figure. She was Superstition.

"I am the strongest in the region of romance," said she,—and she herself believed it.

And the lantern's light gave the lustre of the full moon over the whole earth; yes, the earth itself became transparent, as the still waters of the deep sea, or the glass mountains, in the fairy tale.

"My kingdom is thine! sing what thou see'st; sing as if no bard before thee had sung thereof."

And it was as if the scene continually changed. Splendid Gothic churches, with painted images in the panes, glided past, and the midnight-bell struck, and the dead arose from the graves. There, under the bending elder tree, sat the mother, and swathed her newly-born child; old, sunken knights' castles rose again from the marshy ground; the drawbridge fell, and they saw into the empty halls, adorned with images, where, under the gloomy stairs of the gallery, the death-proclaiming white woman came with a rattling bunch of keys. The basilisk brooded in the deep cellar; the monster bred from a cock's egg, invulnerable by every weapon, but not from the sight of its own horrible form: at the sight of its own image, it bursts like the steel that one breaks with the blow of a stout staff. And to everything that appeared, from the golden chalice of the altar-table, once the drinking-cup of evil spirits, to the nodding head on the gallows-hill, the old crone hummed her songs; and the crickets chirped, and the raven croaked from the opposite neighbour's house, and the winding-sheet rolled from the candle. Through the whole spectral world sounded, "death! death!"

"Go with me to life and truth," cried the second form, the youth who was beautiful as a cherub. A flame shone from his brow—a cherub's sword glittered in his hand. "I am *Knowledge*," said he: "my world is greater—its aim is truth."

And there was a brightness all around; the spectral images paled; it did not extend over the world they had seen. Superstition's lantern had only exhibited *magic-lantern* images on the old ruined wall, and the wind had driven wet misty vapours past in figures.

"I will give thee a rich recompense. Truth in the created—truth in God!"

And through the stagnant lake, where before the misty spectral figures rose, whilst the bells sounded from the sunken castle, the light fell down on a swaying vegetable world. One drop of the marsh water, raised against the rays of light, became a living world, with creatures in strange forms, fighting and revelling—a world in a drop of water. And the sharp sword of Knowledge cleft the deep vault, and shone therein, where the basilisk killed, and the animal's body was dissolved in a death-bringing vapour: its claw extended from the fermenting wine-cask; its eyes were air, that burnt when the fresh wind touched it.

And there resided a powerful force in the sword; *so* powerful, that the grain of gold was beaten to a flat surface, thin as the covering of mist that we breathe on the glass-pane; and it shone at the sword's point, so that the thin threads of the cobweb seemed to swell to cables, for one saw the strong twistings of numberless small threads. And the voice of Knowledge seemed over the whole world, so that the age of miracles appeared to have returned. Thin iron ties were laid over the earth, and along these the heavily-laden waggons flew on the wings of steam, with the swallow's flight; mountains were compelled to open themselves to the inquiring spirit of the age; the plains were obliged to raise themselves; and then thought was borne in words, through metal wires, with the lightning's speed, to distant towns. "Life! life!" it sounded through the whole of nature. "It is our time! Poet, thou dost possess it! Sing of it in spirit and in truth!"

And the genius of Knowledge raised the shining sword; he raised it far out into space, and then—what a sight! It was as when the sunbeams shine through a crevice in the wall in a dark space, and appear to us a revolving column of myriads of grains of dust; but every grain of dust here was a world! The sight he saw was our starry firmament!

Thy earth is a grain of dust here, but a speck whose wonders astonish thee; only a grain of dust, and yet a star under stars. That long column of worlds thou callest thy starry firmament, revolves like the myriads of grains of dust, visibly hovering in the sunbeam's revolving column, from the crevice in the wall into that dark space. But still more distant stands the milky way's whitish mist, a new starry heaven, each column but a radius in the wheel! But how great is this itself! how many radii thus go out from the central point—God! So far does thine eye reach, so clear is thine age's horizon! Son of time, choose, who shall be thy companion? Here is thy new career! with the greatest of thy time, fly thou before thy time's generation! Like twinkling Lucifer, shine thou in time's roseate morn.

Yes, in knowledge lies Poetry's California! Every one who only looks backward, and not clearly forward, will, however high and honourably he stands, say, that if such riches lie in knowledge, they would long since have been made available by great and immortal bards, who had a clear and sagacious eye for the discovery of truth. But let us remember that when Thespis spoke from his car, the world had also wise men. Homer had sung his immortal songs, and yet a new form of genius appeared, to which a Sophocles and Aristophanes gave birth; the Sagas and mythology of the North were as an unknown treasure to the stage, until Oehlenschlaeger showed what mighty forms from thence might be made to glide past us.

It is not our intention that the poet shall versify scientific discoveries. The didactic poem is and will be, in its best form, always but a piece of mechanism, or wooden figure, which has not the true life. The sunlight of science must penetrate the poet; he must perceive truth and harmony in the minute and in the immensely great with a clear eye: it must purify and enrich the understanding and imagination, and show him new forms which will supply to him more animated words. Even single discoveries will furnish a new flight. What fairy tales cannot the world unfold under the microscope, if we transfer our human world thereto? Electro-magnetism can present or suggest new plots in new comedies and romances; and how many humorous compositions will not spring forth, as we from our grain of dust, our little earth, with its little haughty beings look out into that endless world's universe, from milky way to milky way? An instance of what we here mean is discoverable in that old noble lady's words: "If every star be a globe like our earth, and have its kingdoms and courts—what an endless number of courts—the contemplation is enough to make mankind giddy!"

We will not say, like that French authoress: "Now, then, let me die: the world has no more discoveries to make!" O, there is so endlessly much in the sea, in the air, and on the earth—wonders, which science will bring forth!—wonders, greater than the poet's philosophy can create! A bard will come, who, with a child's mind, like a new Aladdin, will enter into the cavern of science,—with a child's mind, we say, or else the puissant spirits of natural strength would seize him, and make him their servant; whilst he, with the lamp of poetry, which is, and always will be, the human heart, stands as a ruler, and brings forth wonderful fruits from the gloomy passages, and has strength to build poetry's new palace, created in one night by attendant spirits.

In the world itself events repeat themselves; the human character was and will be the same during long ages and all ages; and as they were in the old writings, they must be in the new. But science always unfolds something new; light and truth are everything that is created—beam out from hence with eternally divine clearness. Mighty image of God, do thou illumine and enlighten mankind; and when its intellectual eye is accustomed to the lustre, the new Aladdin will come, and thou, man, shalt with him, who concisely dear, and richly sings the beauty of truth, wander through Poetry's California.

THE END.

www.ingramcontent.com/pod-product-compliance
Lightning Source LLC
Chambersburg PA
CBHW030635130626
46552CB00002B/859